EMANCIPATION FROM
SIN'S SLAVERY

EMANCIPATION FROM
SIN'S SLAVERY

How Far Back Do You Have To Go
To Get The Full History?

BILL SINOCK

EMANCIPATION FROM SIN'S SLAVERY
HOW FAR BACK DO YOU HAVE TO GO TO GET THE FULL HISTORY?

Author Credits: William C. Sinock aka Bill Sinock

Certain characters in this work are historical figures, and certain events portrayed did take place. However, this is a work of fiction. All of the other characters, names, and events as well as all places, incidents, organizations, and dialogue in this novel are either the products of the author's imagination or are used fictitiously.

iUniverse books may be ordered through booksellers or by contacting:

iUniverse
1663 Liberty Drive
Bloomington, IN 47403
www.iuniverse.com
1-800-Authors (1-800-288-4677)

Because of the dynamic nature of the Internet, any web addresses or links contained in this book may have changed since publication and may no longer be valid. The views expressed in this work are solely those of the author and do not necessarily reflect the views of the publisher, and the publisher hereby disclaims any responsibility for them.

Any people depicted in stock imagery provided by Thinkstock are models, and such images are being used for illustrative purposes only. Certain stock imagery © Thinkstock.

ISBN: 978-1-4917-4862-6 (sc)
ISBN: 978-1-4917-4863-3 (e)

Printed in the United States of America.

iUniverse rev. date: 11/22/2014

CONTENTS

Special editor and adviser
Chet Ground, MS, Biology
I Sam 19:2 Jonathan delighted much in David

This book is dedicated to the one
hundred persons that after reading this
book finds such inspiration that they seek
after God. He welcomes all seekers.

ACKNOWLEDGMENT

Thanks to God who gave me the inspiration, and to spell check, grammar check, and friend check. Should you find something amiss please let me know, or any other communication.

beijingbill@beijingbill.net

FOREWORD

Wanting the world to be a better place is the driving force behind a great deal of human effort. Sure some only long for profit, but may be this book can rescue them from the fallacy of possessions. This little book, disseminated without cost, is my contribution to humanity's improvement. Yes the book emphasizes Jesus Christ, but the principle is embraced by a majority of the world, believing that somewhere, someone is the savior.

The fact that there is evil in the world cannot be denied, the fact that there is also good, righteous, pure loving elements that could be the predominate ruling factors if more people embraced them is a realistic hope, leading to total monarchal dominance. Freedom, justice, mercy, kindness, honesty, truth, and a concerned love for others are all essential for economic prosperity, political stability and social tranquility. These are God's promoted principles as expressed in the Bible.

May be this book can contribute to that goal.

CHAPTER 1
Sovereign of the Cosmos

Before the beginning, before the universe, before there was matter, light, heat, sound, or a baby's cry, there is God. God occupies all that is, geographically He is in every direction for an eternal distance. How long has He been? There has never been when He was not. There never was a first instant of time, God fills time from eternity past to eternity future. What does God know? Books could be written that fill the Earth, and still books left to fill one hundred Earths. More books to fill more Earths, and still the books would be more, for infinity.

The extreme vastness of empty space is equal to the vastness of God for He fills the vastness and the speck.

God moves from one place to another. There are many places to be and He is in all of them, where each star is He is also. God is in every place, in all places, even places that are not recognized as a place for God alone is aware that that place exists. We created beings, have, but limited mental capacity, and the infinity of God does not fit in our minds. The belief is that God is in three persons is incomprehensible, but then God is incomprehensible, beyond our understanding. The three are one in purpose, in character, and in action. They function in perfect unity as one, so the best we can understand is that there is one. They three are all eternal, self-existing, and in complete harmony. If there is one, three, twenty-three, or a hundred and three the concept would not be more easily understood. How can one paragraph explain God, it cannot.

One God says, "I think we"…followed immediately by another God,… "Should make smaller bodies to accompany the stars," that they had just made… and from the yet unspoken God comes,… "We can make them solid." The thoughts of God, though three, are simultaneously the thoughts of the other two, for each is in the other. From here on God keeps taking turns planning creation. Never a discussion, for what comes out of the mind of one is instantly confirmed by the other two, as there is oneness among them.

God speaks and instantaneously solar systems appear. There may be some processes that take place, but they are so rapid, that the word alone appears to be the total impetus.

Energy, in infinite supply, is isolated in minute specks. The specks of energy repel all the surrounding specks, and at the same time have the quality of attraction giving the energy the characteristics of solid objects. Differing quantities of energy produce solids of different qualities. Combining these give even more variations, making the possibilities infinite.

God puts the solids in orbit around stars. The attraction force keeps the solids from flying off into space, and another force that God causes to function, keeps the solids from crashing into the star as they stay in orbit. The amount of heat energy present changes the solids to liquid and also to a gas.

Energy bursts from God's mouth as He speaks as entire solar systems come into existence with the breath of His voice. When a few billion solar systems circulate about, God takes His finger and starts them all revolving about a central point, where the attraction force is very strong. God sets the rotation at just the speed for the opposing forces to be neutralizing, so all the stars remain in the same place in relation to all others in this spinning platter.

God says, "Some solids are too hot, some are too cold, but others are the proper heat energy for an energy substance to be liquid. This liquid, that is water, is vital for vegetation, and other forms of life that I now design. I now cover these solids with millions of various kinds of vegetation.

This solid I choose as my headquarters. I now have a place where I really can sit. I call it heaven." With God here, heaven is full of love, peace, tranquility, all of His creation shares the same peacefulness.

"Heaven will be an even better place if we populate it with intelligent free beings able to love. The only way for heaven to continue to have love, peace and tranquility is for us to create beings as we ourselves, with freedom to think and do. We will give them wonderful brains, but we will not fill the brains with all knowledge and wisdom. We will let them learn. They will learn all about creation, and we will teach them love."

"If we give them this liberty they could develop ideas of none love." "Yes, that is true, but freedom is the only way for happiness to exist. Freedom of choice to think and do is the prerequisite for love, peace and tranquility to prevail, and all creatures to love one another."

"We make them as much like us as possible. They will not be infinite, they will have a beginning, and they will be created beings."

First God fills the mountains and valleys with millions of various kinds of creatures with diverse levels of intelligence, called animals. They are all care free. Without effort on their part they will serve one another, both creatures and plants symbiotically live to maintain the living environment of all others.

One, if not the first, god like creatures God creates is the angel Lucifer. God's special gift to Lucifer is music. Lucifer can sing in multiple parts. Lucifer is magnificent. Then from the mind, heart and hand of God comes millions of similar God like beings. No two are alike, all have a unique specialty gift that each can be perfecting throughout eternity.

Billions of heavenly creatures are immensely enjoying their lives of whole health happiness. The needs and wants of others is their constant pleasure to provide. Each has the deepest conviction of friendship with all others. Life is filled with companionship, adventure, excitement, and discovery.

With heaven's society established in love, peace, freedom and prosperity, God turns His attention to speaking billions of new planets and stars into existence, and organizing them into star orbiting systems, and those systems orbiting in immense galaxies. Galaxies are then organized into larger units of galaxies in orbit, and those larger units orbiting still larger units, with infinity of expansion.

The heavenly throngs look on in wondering awe. Is it possible for even more to proceed from the hand of the Creator? What marvels await to materialize from the Infinite imagination?

CHAPTER 2

Difference is Paramount

In God's creation all individuals are different from his fellows. Only God Himself shares sameness with the three that are Himself. The three are identical in every respect. If one were to stub His toe, the other two would have an identical toe swelling, given that stubbing God's toe is even possible.

Tranquility prevails until, Lucifer, a free thinking intelligent being contemplates that someone is superior to him that should not be. God gives all the god like creatures all the attributes of Himself, all but infinity, for infinity is something that God alone possesses. Some things are impossible for even God.

For someone to be infinite, they must be present from eternity, and only God has life in Himself.

The three that are one God are together all the time, for even if one is at the other end of the cosmos they are still together for God is omnipresent, that is, in all places at all times. Lucifer begins to think that God is holding out on him, for Lucifer could only be in one place at a time.

When God converses with Himself saying something, the other two know what is spoken as it first originates as thought, because God's mind is three minds functioning as one mind. Each of the three have being in the other two, equal to the manner of being in Himself, three to the power of zero which is one.

God makes all the god like creatures to have independent minds, free to think, explore and create, here to fore, amongst creatures, never before to be thought of concepts. Concepts, of course, not new to God for creatures cannot think a thought that is new to God, for there is nothing conceivable that is beyond God's fore knowledge.

Lucifer could not understand this exclusive unity of mind that the three experienced in unity of mind purpose and function. He wanted to be included in the threesome. Had God given to Lucifer, that which he thought he wanted, Lucifer would have ceased to exist as an independent free thinking person, possessing individuality.

Michael, the arch angel, one of the three of God and Lucifer are best of friends, they have been so sence Lucifer's first conscience thought. Michael sharing with Lucifer all the knowledge and character qualities of God in as great a quantity, and rapidity as Lucifer can comprehend.

Lucifer, first born amongst a multitude of siblings, he is head of all the heavenly beings, choir director, and special Seraph. Seraph, six winged fiery serpents, special attendants to the throne of God. Uncommon metamorphous is required at the times of Seraphim service. Only two Seraphim abide in all of creation, Lucifer and Gabriel, of which Lucifer is the superior.

Lucifer, as chief Seraph is present at all the top three conferences held. Although able to see the meeting take place, he is unable to hear. God's dialogue with Himself takes place at the speed of thought, and only three minds function at their particular frequency.

Lucifer and Gabriel are first to know what God is going to do next, but Lucifer is still plagued with lingering thoughts of why he is excluded.

Lucifer has knowledge, understanding, skills and powers that cause all the other heavenly beings to astonishingly admire him. Michael, his teacher, confident, and best friend is just like himself, but elevated beyond him, why? The more Lucifer thinks about this exclusion the more he believes that there is injustice in God's court. Thinking more and more about this injustice incites feelings of hurt, fostering unhappiness. His mind seethes to the point of anger. The more he thinks the angrier he gets. The angrier he gets the more he thinks about this supposed unjust exclusion.

"If God, Michael and the Spirit will not invite me into the inner sanctum, I will make my own way. I will ascend into to the center of heaven. I will create a throne for myself, and place it above all of God's creatures, even Gabriel. I will sit with authority on the mountain of God, and the congregation of all the heavenly beings will worship before me facing the North. They will be as clouds at my feet. I, to all onlookers, will appear identical to the most high in authority, prestige, and power, yes, Lucifer, like the most high."

Lucifer is absolutely free. Freedom subsists only while basking fully in love. God's mind and purpose is saturated in love. Every thought, word, or action of God is prefaced, embodied, and appendixed with love. All is for the benefit of others. He wants the best for His creatures and He wants His creatures' highest ambition, to be supplying the best for all other creatures. The natural nature of loving citizens in a free society is to be concerned with the wellbeing of others. God knows that doing this will supply all His creatures, all the time with the best of happiness.

Love that enables freedom also enables the possibilities of none loving thoughts, words and actions which distort freedom. God knows to enable freedom opens the avenue to alternate means of living, but freedom being ultimately the superior social system, the hazard of none love is immutable. The loving society is the default society of the cosmos. This situation must be met with intelligent reasoning and evidence, with the absence of any force, coercion, or sleight of hand influence.

God has no choice but to let Lucifer have full reins to work out his scheme. To alter Lucifer in any way; tapping his brain, moving him to a subordinate position, or removing him from existence would replace love with fear, making fear the underpinning of society instead of love.

The two concepts must coexist until to the totality of intelligent god like creatures come to the conclusion, without reservation, that any system deviant from God's is a disaster. Love belongs to God, and God wants love to belong to all His creatures. He does not want His creatures to belong to love, so that, love rules. No, His creatures are to rule, motivated by love, because love is unanimously the intellectual concept held.

Michael tries to reason with Lucifer in the kindest gentlest terms. Michael points out that he is bringing discord among the happiest of people. Instead of looking out for the interests of others, Lucifer's motive is to get all he can for himself. The undisputable end of this philosophy is that each bites his fellows. Many fall at the way side into poverty, as others amass great holdings of wealth. This causes many to suffer from lack of life's necessities, leading to starvation or death at the hand of the wealth grabbers. The process does not stop here, for the greed of possessions, and power catapults the greedy to ever increasing debauchery to eliminate, kill, strangle, and starve the competition. All are the competition, for greed wants all for self. This struggle continues until only two dogs are standing. The winner here gets all, but they shoot each other, and both bleed to death in the lap of luxury.

Michael explains the undesirable outcome in the most humble terms, but Lucifer interprets this humility as weakness. In Lucifer's mind set, he deplores weakness, and sees himself employing the position of strength. He believes that strength will prevail, and he is encouraged that success is in his grasp.

Lucifer, the highest ranking of the god-like created beings is held in highest esteem among the other created beings. Angels frequently come to him with their questions and honor greatly his knowledge and opinion. They trust him; their pleasure is to carry out his commands. Obviously conditions are just right for Lucifer to publicize his designs for improving of heaven's perfection making heaven an even better place.

With Lucifer's plan, heavenly creatures would experience a fuller freedom, freedom that presently they are being deprived. Lucifer brings to their minds that they are under law. The law of love, but they are forced to abide by this law without respect to their own intelligence. After all are they not intelligent and full of love, able to conduct themselves in a loving manner. They need not a law to dictate to them, it is not even possible for them to err in the pursuit of happiness for all.

Amongst these improvements to heavenly society, Lucifer slips in that Michael, the Son of God is held in higher esteem than himself. If he is just made equal with the Son of God he would be able to bring these improvement ideas to God's attention. The future happiness and contentment of all his fellows hinges on his being able to commune with God on an equal par with the Son, to say nothing to the fact, that, this inequity is an injustice, probably perpetrated by the Son himself to secure the greater authority and prestige for Himself.

While displaying the utmost loyalty to God, he stealth fully infests the minds of the peaceful happy heavenly creatures with distrust and discontent. He insists that bringing charges against the Son of God is absolutely necessary to establish the stability of God's divine government. Not only the Son, but now the Father becomes the object of Lucifer's accusations.

God's approach to any situation is to keep computations simple. The most complex problems he explains in the simplest terms. Lucifer on the other hand, in an effort to confuse his fellow beings, congers up the most inconceivable complications he can to the otherwise simplistic situations. To really explain and be understood is to be concise. To be wordy at great lengths, easily accommodates the insertion of misleading and sinister conspiracies.

The charges that Lucifer raises against The Father and Son become the focal point of heaven's attention with several billion individuals, all with IQs in the quadruple digits, talking simultaneously. The throbbing roar fills the city, and the country side trembles with 10 on the Rector scale. The golden streets are in jeopardy of cracking resulting from the tremor generated by the billions of elevated voices.

There is no rock throwing in the streets, but Lucifer displays an emotional outbreak never before seen, "temper." He flails his arms, gestures violently, raises he voice, and grimaces his face with anger and hate. He also invents a new oratory technique, "the bold face lie." He brings charges against the Father and the Son that he knows are not true. That the Father and the Son, though claiming to bestow freedom on all intelligent beings, are really holding out on them.

Lucifer announces with blaring clarity that God alone fully enjoys true freedom. What we, the heavenly beings, are strapped with freedom that is but a faint feeble fraudulent counterfeit.

Many angels embrace Lucifer's accusations, their minds fill with the same discontent, like Lucifer, they display anger. They lose control and lash out in fits of rage.

Not all are taken in by Lucifer. Some angels convey the thought that in fact the Son is the one that created them and gave them life. Surely to esteem the Son higher than ourselves is completely reasonable. He is always fair and kind. He treats all with equality, and there has never been any injustice. The complaints are fabricated on accusation only, no evidence has been presented, but still why do complaints exist? Why, in such a pristine happy environment is there so much disgruntlement and even anger? Puzzling questions linger in the minds of even the stanches of loyal angels.

CHAPTER 3
Diplomacy Before Conflict

In a meeting to discuss the issues in a more tranquil setting, Gabriel takes the podium to speak. Present are, Lucifer along with some of his ardent followers, and Gabriel accompanied by some high ranking angels. Gabriel stands at the podium ready to defend God the Father and Son.

"God desires from all His creatures the service of love; service that springs from an appreciation of His character. He takes no pleasure in a forced obedience; and to all He grants freedom of will, that they may render Him voluntary service. Until this time, for as long as I have existed I have never known there to be any discord. This is the first time I have heard even one word that even suggests questioning God's righteous, loving character. I am well-nigh baffled to hear such words now. Perfect harmony prevailed throughout God's creation as love for one another and God fills ever heart." The meeting disperses with silence hovering over in reverent stillness. Everyone withdrew to their own home in deep contemplation of the proceedings.

Following that is a new moon, when all heaven's angels assemble before God's throne. The angels stand on a miraculous plane. From under the thrones of God flows a river of crystal water. The water forms a lake for many square miles to accommodate the billions of angels gathering there. The water surface tension is increased to the point that it supports enormous weight. The lake takes on the characteristic of solid, but remains water. The billions of angels stand in formation on the solid crystal sea.

Elevated slightly is the rather large stair stepped choir loft with ample room to accommodate a choir of 200 thousand in number. The choir director, Lucifer, stands on a pedestal to the front of the choir.

High above the choir are arranged three golden thrones. The elements about the thrones are molten, as lava, with an occasional outburst of flame like a sun burst. Over the thrones is a rain bow. The rainbow colors are bright, and each band of color is very wide. The bow arch is about a mile from end to end with the thrones centered below. Upon the thrones, sits God. Father God may be sitting in the middle, but that cannot be determined for the three are identical. When one speaks He identifies Himself, then you can tell.

Though some angels are at great distances, there is no focal point at which the view is obstructed. Angel's eye sight is telescopic without difficulty. The most distant angel can pick out his friends in the choir, and watch a hand pluck a stringed instrument in the orchestra.

The worship begins when Lucifer raises his arms, and the choir and orchestra come to the ready. Lucifer commences the tempo, and the choir and orchestra combine to create heart throbbing inspirational music. Lucifer is more in tuned to the music than anyone, after all, under the inspiration of Michael, he composed the music and wrote the lyrics employing his own creativity. The music fills him with peace, contentment and love. Thoughts of love and compassion for all fill his head, and heart. He thinks, "It is true, Michael has been the best of friends, and a wonderful teacher. Michael, The Father, and The Spirit have created a wonderful place, filled with loving people where justice and tranquility prevail. I should quit my complaining and be happy with my job as leader of the angels, after all God has shared everything with me, but... Lucifer skips a beat, the orchestra and choir reflect his error, but Lucifer instantly regains his composure, and the music regains its reverential inspirational quality. And Lucifer thinks, "It's no big deal, I have more than anyone else." With resolve, the spirit of evil departs and love and devotion fills Lucifer's heart, he begins directing the music with more gusto and the orchestra and choir embrace his enthusiasm and the music is even more stirring than ever before. Lucifer keeps directing, but looks up, and catches the eye of Michael. "This is for you, my master and friend" his lips recite.

The music continues for a great duration, and thrills to souls of all and inspires then to greater love and devotion to God, their creator, and greater service to their fellow created angel. The music does come to a finally, and billions angels say amen.

Without haste The Father stands, "Thank you, Lucifer, choir and orchestra for that wonderful inspirational prelude. My gratitude goes out to all of you, thank you for accepting my invitation and assembling here today.

The Holy Spirit, the Son and I are all one in the same. The Holy Spirit is self-existing. The Son is self-existing. And there never was, when I was not. None but the Holy Spirit and the Son can fully inter into the full purpose and designs of the Father.

My Son did all the creating; He created all of you and gave you life. In order to be self-existing means that there never an existence without the self- existing one present. My Son, in giving you life, gave you part of himself. He gave you life that had a beginning, but will never have and ending. You are all my children. Before you is the cosmos with trillions and trillions of galaxies, the cosmos is infinite. Adding to infinity, My Son continues creating more galaxies with home planets where an infinity of happy free children live. Shortly my Son will complete the creation of a new Planet called Earth. The life on this planet will be unlike any thus far created. You are welcome to watch the process.

There is a most accurate explicit definition of the word freedom in your lives. Please hear my Son."

God the Father gestures toward His Son, the elements respond with churning eruptions, sun burses of flame reach out. Several nuclear type explosions occur, but the heat and blast are contained. Attention is focused on the Son.

The Son begins to speak. Pitch, tone quality, inflection and emphasis are so perfectly utilized that the mere sound of His speaking is breath taking. He indeed has the undivided concentrative attention of all. To this wonderful sound the Son adds words of wisdom.

"My wisdom and knowledge are infinite, and I desire to share all with you. As you study and develop through eternity, you will gain more loving characters, more power and freedom to think and do. The more you learn of Me the more like Me you become. My pleasure is that you all become as I am. But you must remember, I am infinite, infinite past, and infinite future, because you have a beginning you will ever have before you more to learn about Me.

CHAPTER 4
Happiness Turned to Turmoil

Lucifer is happier now than he has been for some season. He basks in the enjoyment of his freedom. He is the leader of angels. He is highest in authority, only The Son is higher in authority and then only in a few areas. He brings happiness and cheer to all. Angels all seem to follow his example.

As the Father and The Son presented the circumstances of created life, all were satisfied, as it could be no other way.

While Lucifer improves the happiness of heaven, the Son is making preparations to create the Earth. Many of the planets had differing forms of life and different ecosystems. Earth was to introduce a new concept in life forms, self-procreation. In all other planets all life forms came directly from the hand of the Son. The Earth was to have two separate types of beings within a species. One would have the seed of life, in a single cell, and the other would have the life catalyst, in the form of another single sell. The one to bear the seed will be called Female. The one with the catalyst cell will be called the Male. This procreation system will extend to all forms of life, plant, animal, and man. Man will be the name given to the supreme intelligent creature. Man will rule the Earth.

Of man the male will be somewhat larger and stronger than the female. Man, male and female, will be the most beautiful creatures on the planet. The first man, male and female will be created fully grown, but after that all additional creatures will be nourished inside the female's body until such point of growth the creature can sustain life in the Earth's environment. The young will develop in different ways, many including man will be nourished by their procreation masters. Man's procreation masters, will be called mama and daddy, mama being the female and daddy being the male.

The Son makes all these plans known to heaven and all the planets of the cosmos. Shouts of joy ring throughout heaven and every planet. Angels are exhilarated in anticipation to see the new planet and all the new creatures, especially man.

Lucifer and one of his closest angel friends, one that Lucifer had shared his former ideas for heaven's improvement serendipitously meet. The angel says, "I am happy that all those questions about God's justice and love are behind us. I am happier and I believe that you are happier as well. I have been thinking. I know that I am created. You and many others told me that they witnessed my creation, so I know. All others that I know have witnesses to their creation, but I have never met anyone that says they witnessed your creation, just a thought that occurred to me."

Lucifer left this encounter in a daze. Everything he attempted would go fine for a while, and then the thought of his origin would fill his brain. Am I created or am I really eternal thus equal with the son, and The Father. The Son may have subordinated me to this honored, but subordinate position so He alone could be the creator? Love's courtesy would dictate that The Son would at least consult me concerning the Earth. But He did not even tell me He was doing so.

Not knowing of The Son's plans should have been sufficient evidence that Lucifer was created. Had he been eternal with the Father he would have been as omniscient as the Father, and would know every thought and impulse of the Son.

Lucifer thinks, "I would have been happy just playing a minor roll, but no I am subjected to knowing as everyone else, by public announcement.

All the smooth words of the last general meeting was just a ploy, to shut me up. Well I will not shut up, in fact I will go forth with my plans as before, but in this juncture I will not be dissuaded. I will go forth until I have my objective. I will be like the most high. I will sit on the sides of the North."

Lucifer first finds the angel that he had the conversation about being created or being eternal. Angel, Legion, you got me to thinking, coupled with the latest announcement about Earth, we are being slighted. We are the angels of the Cosmos, certainly, if nothing else, we should be superior to all other godlike creatures. Now God is about to create two new creatures with the ability to create their own kind. We should be able to do that, then we would be creator and ruler of our own race of godlike creatures. Spread the word, if I were restored to my rightful place, so artfully deprived by the trickster Son, angels would be not godlike, but like God.

Lucifer's mind whorls with thoughts of injustice, and soon overwhelming jealousy of The Son seizes his, mind, body and soul. I shall not stand, as a sentry, by God's thrown, but sit next to Him as His equal, and The Son will not convey orders to me, but I will to Him.

The angels chose sides almost as before, but not all, some that had shared Lucifer's sentiments before no longer share them, but stand firm with Gabriel and the loyal angels. Lucifer tells them that they are deluded. "You cannot see the facts before your face. God, Himself, gave you free, reasoning minds, why are you not using them. Gabriel, though I know you are created, I witnessed your creation, you of all angels should admit that The Son is favored over you and me. Justice demands equality."

The discussion, turns into a debate, the debate generates anger, and the first incident of physical confrontation in angel history occurs. The heavenly city is sectioned into corridors of power, Lucifer and his followers occupying one third of the city and Gabriel and the loyal angels occupying two thirds of the city.

Gabriel immediately seeks out The Son. Of course The Son is totally aware of the developments, but Gabriel is seeking advice, what should be done. This is a terrible state of affairs.

The Son accompanies Gabriel, to the loyal sector. Everyone is assembled, the Son begins to speak. "I know there is turmoil in the city. There is also turmoil in your own minds. I understand and none are condemned for having puzzling questions and even doubts about the Father's loving character in dealing with all His children. Accusations have been made against the Father, and only proof will annul these accusations. Bear with the Father and I, for the truth will be made plain only after an extended duration. Lucifer has contrived evil. Evil is life without love, oh, evil does have a deviant love, but not sacrificial concern for others.

Watch, over the long term. Lucifer has created an environment of greed. Greed is where one is interested in self without regard for others. What will happen is that each individual will want to get and not give. Some will rise to power and others will sink into slavery. Even the slaves will fight over what is left. Former companions become competitors, so the desire to eliminate the competition will grow stronger. No one is happy for they only want to grab more. This movement has built-in attributes of self-destruction. Please, be patient, the truth will be revealed."

The Son now starts for the rebel sector. Gabriel and the loyal angles join Him walking over to the rebels. They walk into a churning, chaotic, angry, mob of angels. Every angel begins yelling at the Son, demanding answers, and corrections to the imperfection in heaven's society. Even though thousands upon thousands of demands are directed to the Son simultaneously, he is quite capable of responding to all instantaneously. The angels, having received a thought message addressing their concerns from the Son, begin to quiet down. Then the Son is able to communicate with them audibly.

The Son delivers almost the same speech as he had delivered to the loyal angels, but adds. "You are angry with the Father and I, because of your perceived inadequacies in the Father's character and the way He treats you. I want to bring to your attention that this same anger will shortly be redirected to your closest friends. You will begin to find faults with each other. You will argue, fight and begin the hate your friends. Ultimately you will even loath yourselves for what you have become.

I created you, and gave you life, but you are not clones of me. You, each of you, are your own person. You have individuality; you have freedom the think and do. Your potential for advancement and development is infinite. The Father and I share a wonderful impartial love for each other which we fully share with all of you. You and I are not exactly the same. Life originated with me, all life permeates from me. Life was given to you. You have an origin; I do not have a beginning. You do not have past eternal life, but you do have future eternal life, if you take care of it.

CHAPTER 5
Civil War in the City

The debate continues, not between the two factions, but within the factions. Gabriel, leader of the loyal faction, claims that God is sovereign by the very fact that all life issues from Him. How else can it be? He could make clones of Himself, but then there would only be one person. Problems between individuals would be much easier, for God cannot disagree with Himself. However, He did not do that. He made all of us absolutely independently different from all other individuals. Each of us is free to think and do; even God does not force us. How good can you have it?

A few of the rebels meander unnoticed into the crowd and listen to Gabriel. They are seven in number.

They leave the meeting and walk down the street to a solitary park to have an undisturbed discussion.

One angel blurts out, "I think Gabriel is right. God opens the way for us to learn and develop to be like Him, but we will never be an exact blueprint of Him. He has given life to trillions of godlike, intelligent beings, and all of them have unique individuality. How could He be fairer?"

A second angel replies, "I agree with all that you say, but what is missing? Or is there anything missing?"

"Lucifer says there is, and what he says seems quite logical, at least the part I understand."

A third angel joins in, "I am fully puzzled. I don't think I side with Lucifer, but I am not sure that God has been completely straight-forward with us. I do know that God gave each of us life. He made me; My name is, Majeure, meaning, "An act of God." I am going to stick with Him, and in the future, hopefully, ahhaa, I will understand."

The second Angel says, "Alright, we all think about the same way; the question is, what should we do?"

"I have an idea," A fourth angel speaks, "Lucifer says he promotes freedom. Let's go back to the rebel side and voice our beliefs, even if they disagree with Lucifer. If he really is for freedom, he will disagree with us, but will still treat us as welcome comrades, like him, in search of truth."

They all agree, "Yes, this is a good plan. Let's go, and see what happens."

"Wait, listen, we came over here without being noticed. We have to make our way back to the rebel side unnoticed."

"He's right, let's split up, no more than two angels together. We will meet at Majeure's house."

"Do we have to meet? How about, if upon our return, everyone starts talking to his closest friends. Keep talking whether angels are happy or angry; we shall keep talking until we are directed to Lucifer."

Majeure, instead of traveling directly to the rebel sector, travels a great distance outside the city, and circles around to approach the city from the opposite side. Once inside the city, he makes his way to his neighborhood. Taking a position on a main thoroughfare, he soon is talking with several angels. They are quick to converse with him as the contention between God and Lucifer is on everyone's lips. Simultaneously his friends are doing the same thing in different parts of the city.

Majeure, with a crowd gathered, explains his opinion of the controversy. "God has certainly dealt very kindly with all angels and populations on the myriad of planets. Maybe Lucifer is right about something missing, but whatever it is, it certainly has not interrupted my life, happiness or freedom. Whatever the problem is, it does not seem to be cause to rebel against God."

One of the angels standing by, one most loyal to Lucifer speaks up. "You are being very coy, but I think underneath you are trying to undermine Lucifer. We need to continue this debate in Lucifer's presence." Majeure agrees along with all others.

The entire crowd, now grown to over a hundred, moves down the street accompanied by the roar of dozens of discussion groups debating the problem. They soon arrive at the city square where Lucifer is already in heavy debate with three of Majeure's friends and more than a thousand others.

Lucifer is speaking. "True indeed, God has given us a lot, but he is keeping the best for himself. God has many more powers and abilities that He is not sharing with us. Why? Now He is going to create a race of people he calls humans. They will have the ability to create duplicates of themselves. I do not know how they will do this. God will make two of these humans, one a male and one a female, whatever that means. Being able to procreate is a great power that has not come to us. Why?"

Majeure speaks up, "I agree with Lucifer; God does not seem to be sharing all the capabilities that we certainly are able to handle with our advanced intelligence and wisdom. But is there any one here that God has treated unfairly? Has he made your life miserable, or tortured you? We are having, this demonstration, essentially rebelling against God, and he does not bring fire down upon us to destroy us. This is proof that we really are free. We can even disagree with God. So my real question is, is there anything so unbearable that would cause us to rebel against God?"

"The point is," replies Lucifer, "God is not one hundred percent fair. If I were elevated to my rightful position of authority, I would make angelic society completely fair, and you would enjoy complete freedom."

"Lucifer, you already have more power and authority than any of us," reasons Majeure. "Why not let us ask God to promote me, just a common angel, to be equal with God, and I can work to improve angelic society."

"Majeure, you are just a trouble maker! You cannot even see where God has been unfair to us; how could you possibly correct the problem. Angels, this Majeure is an infiltrator! He is an agent of God; he does not have your best interests at heart. Angels, throw him out!"

A couple of strong angels grab Majeure and forcefully escort him to the corridor separating the loyal from the rebel sectors. Majeure is forced to go to the loyal sector. As he starts to walk away, his closest friends break away from the crowd and walk in the same direction. Then two more angels say, "I think for now I will remain with God," and they walk away. Then two more, and ten more, then hundreds more walk away to the taunting jeers of the rebel angels who already seem to be unwavering in their decision.

As the hundreds of angels reach the loyal sector, Majeure beckons them to gather around. "Fellow angels, I am not fully settled in my own mind about what is happening, and who is right here, God or Lucifer. Lucifer kicked us out for having an opinion differing from his. There may be a problem, but not such a problem that would cause me to declare war on God. I would like to suggest that we go to God's loyal angels as we did to the rebels. We will stimulate as much serious thinking as we can."

Another angel suggests, "There may be some loyal angels that will believe that we are enemies of God and try to kick us out of the loyal sector."

Majeure replies, "You are right; let's keep up our questioning until that does happen. Then we will let our true purpose be known, that we are only testing their tolerance for freedom. Finally we will encourage all to join us to meet with Michael. At least we will know where the other angels stand. We may even find that a good many of them feel the same as ourselves. I cannot figure, in my own mind, how we will know and fully trust where God stands in regard to the accusations against Him. He has to prove that Lucifer is wrong, and that He, Himself, is fully righteous, has been in the past, and will be in the future."

CHAPTER 6
Negotiate With Michael

"I think we should go to Michael," suggests one of the angels. "We can bring all of our questions to Him and see how He reacts to Lucifer's complaints against Him."

Another asks, "How can we really ask Him a question? He knows what we are talking about, even now."

Majeure answers, "What you say is true, but he does not make us have a question that isn't ours, nor does He prevent us from asking a question that could be hard to answer. He already knows our questions, but we do not know his answer. Let's ask all the questions, and bring up all the arguments that Lucifer presents, and we will use the harshest of terms when we ask. Lucifer kicked us out; what will Michael do?"

The large group of angels heads toward the city center where Michael can be found. At first, the group of angels is largely made up of those that had joined the rebels for a short time, but as they move toward the city center more and more angels join. Some angels are skeptical of Michael, others inquisitive, and some are confident of Michael's loving response.

A large crowd is gathering, well-nigh half the loyal city, and the other half is on its way. This encounter is of great consequence to all.

As the crowd approaches Michael, Majeure stops and reminds the angels, "We were courteous to Lucifer, yet held back no question. Let us do the same with Michael."

With the billions present, Michael is encouraged to ascend to a platform so all can see as well as hear. Hearing is not a problem for Michael has a perfect speaking voice, and the angels have perfect hearing, but they need line of sight in order to see. The meeting could certainly last for an extended duration with the possibility of millions of questions, but with eternity available, no one is concerned.

Majeure approaches from the former rebels, and Gabriel represents the loyal angels. The former rebels have lots of questions, but the loyal angels have their questions as well.

Majeure speaks first, "We all admit that you have been very patient with Lucifer. We have discussed that you could just take life from Lucifer or any one that does not agree with you, yet you do not. We just had a conversation with Lucifer. Lucifer kicked me out just for disagreeing with him. Many others, thousands of thousands, joined me as I left, and we have seen your patience. Lucifer says that your long-suffering is evidence of your weakness, and his steadfastness is proof of his strength. He believes that we should just remain with him, and you will ultimately come to terms with us, making us free indeed. However, I am not sure just what freedom I and the others are missing. Certainly you can see, if we believe we are missing something that you are withholding, then we doubt the truth of your words. Would you please address this problem for us."

All eyes and ears are centered on Michael as He begins to speak. While Majeure was speaking, many small groups were haggling over the situation, but all that stops, for all want to hear Michael.

"There have been many accusations brought against My Father and Myself. One is true, My Father, the Holy Spirit, and Myself are eternal. We make up the sovereign authority of the cosmos. Before there was star, planet or angel, before there was the vacuum of empty space, We are."

"We created matter and the natural laws that govern their function. We created all the various plants, and then all the lower creatures, establishing an ecosystem where all that lives aids in sustaining the ecosystem of life. When all was ready for you to have a harmonious habitat, we made angels."

"Angels were designed after ourselves, but we did not mass produce angels, each and every one of you was hand-crafted. Each of you is unique from his fellows. No two of you are exactly alike. Love was our motivating principle in making you, for love fills the heart of God, and we filled your hearts with love."

"You were given brains with superior intellect, physical bodies of immense strength, and you function in the physical and the spiritual universe. You have absolute freedom to think and do. Love is your guiding principle, for divine wisdom knows that any endeavor, outside of love, will self-destruct."

"Your life will know no end. You were given a life with an eternal future. You do not have an eternal past for you had a beginning. God wants you to be like Him, and He has placed before you the entire cosmos, all of His divine wisdom, and loving character. The more you learn of Him, the more power you will be given. Will you ever be exactly the equal with God? No. When you have learned of God, and gained vast knowledge and enormous powers, you will have yet before you an eternity of further expansion of your knowledge and powers."

"Lucifer has made accusations against God. The truth or falsehood of these accusations is not such that claims or counter claims are of much value. The truth will be revealed by demonstration. God's love will be demonstrated, making very clear the truth or error of Lucifer's claims. Lucifer will reveal, by his own actions, his true character. This process will require patience for all your questions to be answered. I plead with you to remain with God and give this process time to work."

"For now, if you would, go to your friends in the rebel sector, go to them and tell them what I have told you. You cannot force or threaten them with any harm. They must make up their own free minds. Stay in the rebel sector until you feel the ground shake. Once you feel the ground shake, come, at once, back to this part of the city. If your home is in the rebel sector, gather up your belongings, and bring them with you. You will be given a new home. If your friends come back with you, wonderful, if they choose not to come, that is their decision, but you leave at once and return here."

"God will not allow rebellion to tarnish the happy society of heaven. The rebel sector of the city will be transported to another planet. Not a sub-planet, but one with all the beauty and amenities as heaven."

"All the rebels will have free access to you who remain in heaven, but only at the city square under this new tree that you see. If any of you changes his mind, and wants to follow Lucifer, just eat one of its fruit, and your intentions will be understood by all. Otherwise do not even taste the fruit of this tree, it is called the tree of Knowledge of Good and Evil. Whoever eats this fruit joins Lucifer."

Almost all of the angels went immediately to the rebel sector to talk to as many as would listen. Some went to their homes to gather their furniture and personal items. Being exceptionally strong, carrying all their belongings in a single trip was of no difficulty for them.

Small groups formed everywhere. At first the conversations were cordial, but as some angels decided to give God a chance, serious rebels begin to angrily blurt out recriminations. "You are delusionary." "You have given your mind over to tyrannical control." "God says he gave you freedom, but you have submitted yourself to slavery." "Your IQ is slightly above that of an Orangutan, well, maybe equal."

The haggling continues for quite a while, but then everyone feels the street beneath their feet slightly vibrate. Some of the loyal angels start back toward their part of town, and a few of the rebel angels decide to join them. Then the jeers really start. Loyal angels surround the former rebels to protect them. Then out of nowhere comes a lightning bolt. It strikes an angel on the calf muscle, swinging his body high in the air and slamming him on the street. As he lies on his back looking up, he exclaims, "I have never experienced anything like that!" Angels help him up, and as they do bolts of lightning start flying everywhere. The lightning is thrown at the speed of light, but the angels are quick to dodge every one, or reflect them with the palm of their hand, harmlessly into space. The shaking intensifies, and the angels, under a barrage, make haste to the loyal part of the city. Rebel angels do not follow them, but keep up the barrage of lightning.

The shaking continues, and soon cracks begin to appear along the street. Then, slowly at first, the entire rebel-held city begins to lift. Picking up speed, raising into the clouds, now moving at stellar speed past stars and galaxies', the huge chunk of heavenly real estate is whisked off to a corner of the universe.

The rebels are terrified, and yell out, "Revenge of the Tyrannical Trinity." However, no one is harmed, as that part of the city containing several billion rebel angels is transported to another planet in a different galaxy from heaven. The city space ship gently descends and settles down on an exquisitely beautiful planet. The rebels do not have to repair or build a single thing. The city's functionality is preserved, and the new environment is pristine. The facilities, buildings and houses are far more than needed to accommodate the population of angels.

Back in heaven there is a gaping cavern one third the size of the entire city. There is an acute housing shortage because many angels have lost their homes that were in the rebel sector. Being resourceful angels, as they are, they immediately begin a reclamation project.

Instead of filling in the new mid-city canyon and building on it, they decide to fill it in with sparking water, creating a large tree-lined lake. Angels move out the existing walls of the city and begin building new homes and convenience facilities for the now homeless angels. With billions of willing and able workers, the construction project proceeds rapidly, and all angels soon have beautiful, luxurious homes.

Even though the rebels' new planet is a five-star resort, there soon begins bickering. They were angry when the transport began, but fear soon conquered and left them terrified. Anger returned when the cause for fear diminished. Angels argue over who should be able to occupy some of the empty homes. "I want this home," "No, I get it, I live next door, and I will knock out a wall and expand my place."

As an angel takes over a new place, he throws all of the unwanted items out into the middle of the street. Soon, a huge pile is blocking the way of anyone wishing to pass by. On-looking angels watch what he is doing.

They loudly object, "You cannot just dump this stuff in the middle of the street!" "Of course I can," he answers. "I am free to do as I please." "Who will clean it up?" they ask. "I do not know, and I do not care! It is not my problem," he retorts, stomping back into his new home.

Everywhere one walks throughout the city, rubbish is piling up in the street. Two angels are walking along, "I never saw this sort of thing in heaven." observes one. "Look, it is more than just these piles of stuff." He kneels down and removes a bit of dirt exposing a spot on the street. "Look, under this dirt is the same burnished, golden shine as back in heaven. What makes the difference?"

His companion replies, "Back in heaven volunteer angels cleaned and polished the streets, and besides, no one made a mess as you see here. Here no one wants to do for others, so work like cleaning the streets never gets done."

In a nearby park, a group of angels gather as two of them argue, each claiming that they have the superior intellect to run the city government. Through the park runs a stream. One angel, while listening to the ego belching debate notices something strange. "Hmm," He thinks to himself, "What is that trashy looking stuff floating down stream?" Then he blurts out for all to hear, "We do not need great intellect to run the city; we need someone willing to keep it cleaned up."

Another angel speaks, "This new self-freedom that ignores the needs of others has its problems. I have seen two angels fight over which one would go through a door first. Others argue about everything. This place is turning into a pit."

Another angel agrees, "Yes, a bottomless pit of trash. Bottomless Pit, that is the name of this city, Bottomless Pit. Welcome to Bottomless Pit. I think I would like to go back to heaven."

"Me too!" chorus his companions. Many others are of the same opinion. A large crowd assembles, and resolves to seek out Lucifer to see what he thinks about the situation. An angel named Legion speaks for the crowd. "Lucifer, we believed you and followed you, but the situation in our city of absolute freedom is not what we were expecting. New things have been introduced; greed, disrespect, and slothfulness. We have come to ask, "What are the possibilities of returning to heaven?"

Lucifer holds up his hand, "You think I am going to be angry with you, but no, I am not. In fact, I agree with you. All my plans are not working out. Even though I made all kinds of lying accusations against Michael, I know he is reasonable, and kinder than any of us realized. I will go to him and ask to be reinstated. I am the leader of this rebellion. If Michael reinstates me, He will do likewise for the rest of you. Stay here; I will be back."

Lucifer flies at 200 times the speed of light and arrives at heaven. He descends onto the city square, and stays under the large tree appointed for him. He tries to speak to passing angels, but none stop; they just continue on their way. Finally after trying to talk to angels, as they walk away, Lucifer yells out, "If you will not talk to me, at least tell Majeure that I would like to speak to him. Lucifer waits for a long while, and then he sees Majeure coming.

"Majeure, I, I am so glad to see you." Lucifer can sense the reluctance and distrust of Majeure. "Wait, wait, I am not here to try to persuade you, argue or lie to you. PLEASE, I need your help."

"Michael has placed us on a planet every bit as beautiful as heaven, and He does not interfere in any way with our lives there, but maybe that is the problem. The "get for yourself" attitude that I thought was so great has turned to greed, disrespect, and slothfulness. Many angels are quite disappointed with the outcome. Many, including myself, would like to be readmitted to heaven and give up our rebellion of supposed improvement on God's ideals. Could you, PLEASE, ask Michael if I could meet with Him on behalf of many of the angels, and maybe if we can work something out. This is not just my idea, for many angels have asked me to represent them."

"My, that sounds like good news to me," answers Majeure. "I will ask Michael and then return to you."

Majeure Seeks out Michael, who is conversing with a number of other angels, so Majeure listens in to the conversation and waits his turn to speak. After many interesting topics are discussed, Majeure gets his turn. "Michael, Lucifer is at the city square under the tree you appointed for him to communicate with us angels. He does have a hard time, for few angels will give him any attention. An angel did convey a message to me that Lucifer wished to speak to me, so I reluctantly went to see what he wanted. Lucifer says that he and some other angels are not happy with the current state of affairs. He admits that he was wrong and that he conjured up lies about you. He asked me to ask you if you would meet with him."

Majeure's words are heard by many angels, and as he speaks more gather and listen with intense interest. When he ceases speaking the crowd has grown to an assemblage.

Michael begins to speak. A hush blankets over the crowd of angels as every ear swells to get Michael's every word. "Of course I will speak with him, My, oh, My, I certainly would have preferred to have him come to this conclusion much earlier. Yes, let us go to meet with Lucifer."

Michael leads the way, down the street, over an arched bridge traversing a river, turning on to the Avenue of Heaven which leads to the city square. As the already large gathering hastens along, the numbers double, and then double again.

Lucifer can now see Michael and the multitude of angels accompanying him. Trepidation enters the heart of Lucifer; he thinks, "Oh, no! What have I got myself into? Is this a lynch mob ready to hang me from this tree?" He is relieved as Michael approaches and greets him with a smile.

"Lucifer, what is on your mind?" "Michael,… I," Lucifer pauses, looks at the ground, shuffles his feet, and then looks at the multitude of angels, making eye contact with all of them. His gaze sweeps the crowd until his eye comes around again to Michael. "I was all wrong. I was jealous of you. I had more than anyone else, but I felt jilted by not being totally equal with you."

In a voice filled with love, Michael responds, "Lucifer, you understand that all angels have the opportunity to learn and grow in knowledge, wisdom and understanding of God's love. The more they do this, and the more they embrace the character of God, the more power they will have. That same process, even though you are much more advanced than all other angels, the infinity of God was fully available to you. Love must precede power, or power could be misused."

"I know," says Lucifer. "I saw the power, and I coveted it, but I am ready to abandon my wrong course of action; just reinstate me in my old job."

When Michael hears these words come from Lucifer, He immediately turns His back, and begins to sob.

As Michael continues sobbing, Lucifer thinks to himself, "It seemed such a request would make Michael happy, why is He carrying on so?"

Michael finally turns back slowly and faces Lucifer. "Lucifer, Lucifer," tears permeate every word. "You have gone too far. You have filled yourself with anger, hate, and lying. These have become part of you. I am sorry Lucifer, you have damaged yourself."

"Are you telling me that I will never be readmitted to heaven?"

"I am saying that you have set your course, and I cannot change it without violating the very precious principle of freedom, which with the respect of all these standing by, I will not do."

Lucifer is seizes with anger. His face twists with hate, and his eyes are aflame with revenge. "If that is the way it is, I will do all in my power to destroy every bit of your creation. I will take you, heaven, and all the planets with me. My demise will be laced with pleasure as I see the rest of you burn in hell with me!"

Lucifer, with his superior power, knocks the first few rows of angels to the ground; then he whirls around, and with a strike of his fingers, starts the tree on fire. Michael sees that Lucifer is just going to keep this up, so he instantly creates a bubble. The bubble glides over to Lucifer and envelops him.

Lucifer keeps on fighting, but he is harmlessly contained in the bubble, and can do no further damage. Michael grabs a handle on the bubble with one hand, and as if from a giant slingshot, hurls the bubble into space toward the planet Bottomless Pit.

Lucifer lands softly on Bottomless Pit, witnessed by the entire population of Angels. At first they shy from the bubble, but soon come over to investigate. Lucifer screams in anger and frustration, "Get me out of here!"

The angels try, but the bubble does not pop like a soap bubble. After sawing, drilling and chopping they finally gouge out a hole large enough for Lucifer to crawl through.

As soon as Lucifer is freed, angels eagerly ask, "How did the meeting go? What happened?" Shaking with fury, Lucifer snarls, "Just leave me alone!" he walks away, and is nowhere to be found.

A large crowd of angles remain after bailing Satan out of the bubble, "Well, it did not go well, considering that reaction. I was in hopes Michael would at least take all the stupid jerks like you." "What do you mean stupid, it's filthy mouthed lame brains like you are what gives this place a bad name." "We need to subdivide this city like we did heaven, the lazy smelly ones all in one section." "Ya, and the dirty mouthed empty heads in the other." A third angel inters in, "I hate it here, everybody are such jerks. You should put me in charge." "Yes, I vote to put you in charge….. of the latrine, you are well qualified for that duty." All around angels are arguing, most in competition to see who can come up with the most ingenious put down.

Finally Satan shows up. "Shut up, you idiots. This is the way it is going to be, I am in charge, what I say goes." "Oh, That sounds like freedom. Satan I hate all these angels and you are the worst of the lot, why don't you just go to hell." "Angel, listen to me, I am already in hell, and you are here with me. Hell is not a place, it is a condition. Look what this place was when we got here and look at it now. I vomit to think that I am going to have to be in the same place with you forever. That is enough to drive me to ask God for execution to replace this incarceration." "You are right Lucifer, now Satan, this hell is the birth place of lies, corruption, filth, deceit, abomination, and some body will come up with ways to make it even worse.

"I thought this was The Pit, but no it's worse, it's hell. I think I will go to another planet and cause them to rebel. I will make myself king." "Angel you can try, but know that God has limited us to go to only The Tree of The Knowledge of Good and Evil when trying to communicate with other worlds. I was in heaven for several new moons before I got to talk to anyone in heaven. Angels just ignored me."

CHAPTER 7

New Kids in the Universe

For an extended period Lucifer remains in solitary. Many of the rebel angels are in bewilderment as to what happened and what will happen next. Finally Satan comes out of self-induced solitude. Angels gather near him, but none utter a word. Lucifer begins to speak. "Our course is set. The door of return is closed forever. We have no option, but to oppose God, and try to conquer more of His creation. Michael is going forth with His plans to create a world and fill it with a new kind of intelligent creatures called human. All of God's family will be watching the creation of this new planet. I think we should pay very close attention.

Lucifer, the rebel angels and all of God's loyal family do not have to wait long for Michael quickly goes into action. Knowing that all are watching and this planet is to be a lesson book to the universe, Michael takes the creation in slow steps, so all can observe.

The sun and all the planets are in place in their orbits around the sun. The system is in darkness as the sun had not yet been kindled. Michael wants to get started and he also wants the angels and dwellers of the other planets to be able to watch, so the first thing that He does is to bring light to the system of dark planets. The light, illuminates up the orbits of all the planets clear out to Uranus and Pluto. Great attention is given to the blue planet called Earth. After making the light he announces that this is the first day.

Angels discuss, the planetary system a little, "Are the animals and these new, humans, all going to be aquatic? The whole planet is a big sea." No one has an answer, but the big question, on the minds of angels is, the new term, "Day." "What is this "day," never heard of it."

Next the angels watch Michael. Michael stirs some of the water. He stirs the water faster and faster. Soon a layer of water rises up and separates from the main body of water. The layer of water, though at a low altitude is moving fast enough to be in orbit. Michael stirs even faster and the water rises in altitude until there is a considerable distance between the water below and the water in orbit. Once this space is established, Michael mixes some chemicals in vapor form. The atmosphere is made up of gaseous nitrogen, oxygen, carbon dioxide and a few other chemicals. They are all in just the right proportions to be perfect for life on the planet. After completing this project Michael announces, "This ends the second day."

Observing angels discuss what they just saw, and one says, "I wonder what He will do on the third day?" "I do not know, but I am going to be here to find out."

When Michael resumes His work, the Earth begins to tremble. Large waves begin to crash around on the great planetary sea. Then the solid part of the planet begins to show above the water level. The solid rises higher and higher, and all over the planet solid substance is seen above the sea. There are many solid parts protruding above the sea. There are many solid areas, some large some small in all parts of the planet with the churning sea rocking between them. Michael says, "The solid part is called land and the water, sea."

Great rivers of water are rushing off the land down to the sea. In some places water is trapped, and cannot make its way to the sea. The land is various colors of brown, to red and some yellow, but something very strange is taking place. The brown ground is turning green. The green, on close examination are millions of plants. First there are plants growing just on the ground, then some plants stick up a little with flowers, then taller plants, and still taller trees until there are towering trees reaching almost to the clouds in the atmosphere. The moment prior, waist land, is now a magnificent lush garden with forest, meadows, rivers and lakes. The sea also is adorned with flora and fauna, waving friendly gestures as the water ebbs and flows, but no creatures to entice. On all the plants are flowers and on most, are also many kinds and colors of fruit. "All this is very good, thus ends the third day."

"I still do not fully understand what a day is, but I am sure going to be here for day four."

Michael snaps His fingers and holds His hand near the sun, and the sun is kindled. First a small part, but a chain reaction is started, and in all direction the fire spreads, and soon the entire planet is ablaze. Light and heat is permeating throughout the entire planetary system. The light and heat radiates out in three dimensional directions, first lighting and warming the innermost planets. The light takes, but a very short part of the day to reach Earth, but a greater part of the day to reach the outer planet Uranus. The satellite, called the moon was already orbiting the Earth, is white in color and very smooth, so it reflects light very well. When the moon is on outer edge of the Earth's solar orbit it lights up the dark part of the Earth's day called night. From the night half of the Earth's day the stars and galaxies are more easily visible. The Earth being tilted in relation to the plane of its orbit makes for varying degrees of light and heat to strike the Earth which creates a situation of different seasons. In this way the days could be understood, a dark portion and a light portion. One full year could be discerned by a repeat of the seasons, caused by the Earth completing an orbit around the Sun. Thus the fourth day comes to an end.

"Watch, on day five Michael will create creatures." "Yes, but what creatures?" "I am not sure, but I am going to be here early to follow closely behind Michael to see what He does."

Very early in the morning Michael is busy at work. Very small creatures about the size of dust start darting vigorously in the water. The creatures appear at one point, but at something less than the speed of light they radiate spreading throughout the entire planet's seas.

There are creatures that just sit where they are; others walk around on the bottom. Then tiny fish appear, then larger, as the process continues larger and larger fish come on the scene, first water breathing fish then air breathing mammals, ending with the finale, great giant whales. The seas are fully populated. The inland lakes and rivers receive the same creative possess. The food supply is extravagantly abundant in the garden of the sea, so no creature is forced to kill for survival. The plants are happy for the pruning because constant new growth needs the room.

Michael comes up out of the sea, and gains altitude in the atmosphere. With microscopic accuracy, Michael designs the feather. A feature needed for His next step. These next creatures are very closely related to the fish just created, for maneuvering in air is very similar to maneuvering in water. Similar, but not exactly the same, for flight creatures have no buoyancy as fish, but must have lift. The lift comes from a unique feature of the wing.

Birds start coming from the hand of Michael. First, short winged birds with large tail stabilizers for very quick maneuverability, then long lanky bodied birds with exceptional wing span for effortless long distant flight. Then birds with all kinds of in between features, large birds and small, begin fluttering off. The final bird to come from Michael's hands is a helicopter bird. This bird has wings that flap faster than an eye blink. The bird can hover; fly forward, backwards, up and down, and sideways. The fifth day culminates with squadrons of birds flying across the sun as it sets, ending day five.

At sun rise on the sixth day there is a moo sound, then a roar, and a meow. Michael makes all the forest, jungle, plane and mountains astir with animals partaking of their first meal. Around a lake a lion, lamb and elephant bend for or reach for a drink of water. In a nearby meadow; a horse, deer and antelope vibe for first place in a hoof race. To show that big does not possess preference, Michael fills the undergrowth and grass with Mosquito, Nat, and Grasshopper. Millions of variations of crawly creatures some winged, some four, six and eight legged, some with two eyes, others eight, and still more with hundreds of eyes, all these tiny creatures meander through the foliage.

Fruit, nut and leaf are in great abundance, supplying food for beast and bug alike. No prey nor be preyed upon can be found for all are happy to feast on the abundant plant life. Like in the sea, consumption just provides room for new growth.

Common to land and sea, all the creatures have a counterpart, an individual that they relate to like they relate to no other on the whole planet. Michael labels those pairs, male and female. When these pairs get together they have the power to create small creatures identical to themselves. Michael blesses this fruitful phenomenon, and says, "fill the earth with your kind."

At this moment a light on the Earth intensifies a thousand times. The Father and the Holy Spirit join Michael on the Earth. They all simultaneously say, "Let us make man in our image." The three work together, first isolating calcium from the soil and form the frame work of man, the bones. Then one works on the arteries, veins, nervous system and brain. The second, forms and attaches muscles in various configurations to provide strength and mobility, and attaches nerve endings to the muscles, so the brain, the command center can control needed movement. The third, constructs and installs all the organs, glans, limp system, and all the vital chemicals. He also makes eyes for seeing and ears for hearing. The lifeless body is complete being covered with smooth skin, having hair in various places serving functionality and appearance. Then they fill the body with life giving blood. All is ready. The Father and the Holy Spirit now look at each other, and say, "We want you, Michael, to breathe life giving spirit into this brand new male human," "My, thank you, for such an honor."

Michael takes the magnificent body into His arms, and cradles the head. He leans forward placing His mouth on the mouth of the yet lifeless form. He exhales, filling the body's lungs with oxygen and some of His own spirit. Spirit permeates through the body; to the heart which begins pumping, then the brain starts waking up the entire body. A slight murmur comes, a wake up stretch, and eyes open. Man's first sight is that of the kind face of Michael, looking down on man's brand new conscience self. Man is helped to his feet. He has complete mastery of a language, but still everything is new to him.

Michael introduces Himself, "I am Michael, this is my Father and yours, and this is the Holy Spirit, an ever present, champion. We created you. What is your name?" "My name? I know! My name (stuttering ah, ah) name is Adam, Yes! That is my name. My name is Adam." Michael takes Adam by the hand. "Come with me Adam, I will show you where you live." Michael and Adam take a walk around the garden.

First Michael and Adam come to a tree with broad speeding branches. The trunk is too large for even for Adam to reach around. Up the trunk is a smaller vine, growing up in to the tree and inter twining around its branches. Hanging down just above Adam's head is a bunch of purple fruit, beautiful to the sight. Michael picks the bunch, separates part, and gives Adam part. "Here try them they are very delectable." "Try them, What does that mean?" Michael eats some and Adam gets the hang of it and he eats one. "Yes, you are right, these are delicious. I will call them grapes for they are fruit of the vine." Michael and Adam continue on their walk eating grapes. As they come to single out a particular plant Michael describes the plant, and they taste its fruit and Adam gives it a name. As they walk and talk Adam gives names to all the plants as he learns of them.

Walking on a little further they come to a humongous artesian well. The flow is voluminous and steady, but not a torrent. The water spout is above Adam's head, but falls back to a level equal to the surrounding water. Adam calls the falls, Eden Water. The water swirls around for a time, and then flows into one of four rivers. Michael explains that this river flows to Havilah, a land where there is much gold and other precious gems. "I will call this river Pison for this river proudly spreads water to the good land. The second river Michael says this river flows all though out the land of Ethiopia. "This river will be called Gihon for this river gushes forth." Adam gives names to the other two rivers just as he names everything he sees. They continue on exploring and naming river, plant and rock.

Michael tells Adam that he is the ruler of all that he sees. "You are in full authority here, and the responsibility to care for plant, animal, river and rock.

All is in your control. You can eat the fruit of all the trees in the garden, with the exception of one. Come let me show you." Michael takes Adam to the center of the garden. There is a meadow there with two majestic trees growing with plenty of space for each.

"This first tree is the tree of the Knowledge of Good and Evil. This tree, although it has fruit, you are not to eat of the fruit of this tree. Eating the fruit of this tree will lead to destruction and death. There are two trees here. You must know each tree, do not get them mixed up. This one, the Tree of The Knowledge of Good and Evil is the tree to avoid. This second tree in the meadow is The Tree of Life. Not only are you free to eat the fruit of this tree, you must eat this fruit to have life that continues on forever, thus its name, Tree of Life."

"Now which tree is which?" "The one we are standing next to is the Tree of Life. The one over there," Adam points, "is the Tree of The Knowledge of Good and Evil." "Well said Adam, best to just stay away from that tree."

Then Adam notices an animal in the meadow with its head reaching down to the ground. "What is that," Adam asks. "That, Adam, is your next job. That is an animal of which there are many hundreds. Let's go and take a closer look." Adam walks over to the animal. He puts his hand to his chin and looks at the animal top to bottom. Then he walks to the other side, and looks up at Michael. "I believe that this animal will be called, Cow." "Excellent" says Michael, "Cow it is." All the land animals are caused to parade one by one, or one might say two by two, before Adam, and to each Adam gives a name.

A little distant from the garden is a great sea. Michael says, "Come with me, we will do something that you have never done before, swim in the sea." Without any diving gear Michael and Adam dive into the sea. Michael is an expert swimmer, and Adam soon gets the hang of it. Going down into the depths of the sea Adam sees all the sea plant, fish and mammal life. The first encounter is with a fish that is bigger than both of them put together. The fish has swept back dorsal and tail fins. The nose is pointed and the mouth is from ear to ear, and is lined with hundreds of razor sharp teeth. "I will call this fish the Oratory Fish for it has a great mouth piece. This fish will be known as the Shark Attorney for it is sly and can represent the other fish. The name can be Shark for short. Then Michael and Adam hitch a ride with an even bigger fish like creature. Swims like a fish, but must come to the surface to breath air. This animal is very big, but is very gentle. As the three travel along the animal keeps eating all along the way. Adam thinks, "This animal has a colossal appetite, He can eat a whale of a lot. Adam blurts out. "That's it." "That's what," Michael asks. "This animal eats a whale of a lot of food. I will call him Whale."

Michael and Adam stay under the water for an hour or two naming all the fish, mammals, and the plants also. Michael takes Adam by the arm, "We have one more area to investigate and name the creatures." They start to ascend. When they arrive at the surface there is no hesitation, they just keep raising into the air. What excitement for Adam, it is his first time to fly.

They continue to gain altitude. The view is fantastic. Adam can see clear to the horizon. The trees below are not tall at all. He can see the head waters of the four rivers, and how they flow out to the horizon, shrinking to a thin line and vanishing at the horizon. Gliding between the clouds, Adam sees a new, yet before unseen, creature. The creature is also gliding among the clouds. "That is a bird, he is the highest flier of birds. That bird is majestic, strong and fearless. The name best fitting for him is high flying Eagle. Eagle shall be the name of this most majestic bird."

Michael and Adam descend to a lower altitude, and while descending they encounter numerous high fliers. Adam names them all; Condor, Falcon, Hawk, Osprey, Crane, gull, Pelican, and Argentavis, the largest of birds. Closer to the ground are; Sparrow, Owl, Parrot, and myriads of others. Adam names them all.

Michael and Adam now land in an exceptionally beautiful part of the garden. "Well done, Adam, you have named all the species on the Earth." "Michael, I did notice one thing, all the animals seem to have a twin, well, maybe not twin, but look alike friend. Do I have a look alike friend somewhere, and we just have not seen them yet?" "No, Adam, The look a likes are the female of the species. Your special friend has not yet been created, but from the very beginning the plan was for you to have a very special companion. You will love her. She will be the most beautiful of all. She will be very close to you. You will be as one person for she will be made of your bone. I am going to put you to sleep and when you awake you will meet her for the first time. Lie down on this very nice comfortable grass."

While Adam is asleep Michael reaches in the side of his chest, separates one rib and pulls it out. From Adam's rib Michael forms the female, taking even more care for perfection then He did with Adam, and Adam is perfect. The female will be even more perfect.

Michael breaths the breath of spirit and life into the female just as He did to bring Adam to life. The female awakes slowly, and takes the hand of Michael, offered to her. She stands beside Michael and asks, "Who is that?" She sees Adam asleep just behind Michael. "He is handsome. He sleeps so peacefully. Can I wake him?" "Of course, he is Adam your husband. He will like you to wake him up, go ahead, wake him."

The female takes her first step, and kneels next to Adam. She takes his hand and lifts it to her bosom. Still holding his hand, she takes one hand and strokes Adam's forehead, running her finders through his hair. Adam then makes a murmur, and slowly opens his eyes. As his vision clears a big broad smile sweeps across his face. He sits up still holding her hand. You are my special companion.

Adam sees her beautiful face with sparkling eyes, and pearly white teeth compassed by her ruby lips. He has never felt this sensation, he is influenced by a very strong impulse to move very near to her and move his lips close to her lips, but he has just met her and he is too shy to be so bold. "You are Eve for you will be the matriarch of the human race."

Michael, Adam and Eve have a luscious dinner of fruit and nuts. Then Adam notices that the Sun is touching the horizon, in fact half of the Sun has already vanished. "What is happening? I have never seen the Sun vanishing before." "Do not worry Adam. The Sun is ending one day and beginning another. In a short time darkness will cover the Earth, and you will see stars and the moon. Sleep will overcome you and you will awake to the new day. Tomorrow is a special Holy Day. We will spend the whole day together. Sleep now and take your rest.

Michael leaves and the two are left alone. "Eve, you will like it here. The garden is a beautiful place, Michael is so very kind. This is the first time we will have a tomorrow, I wonder what it will be like?"

Eve lies down on some very plush grass and bunches up a little for a pillow. Adam lies down beside her taking special care not to touch her. Eve reaches over taking Adam's hand and caresses it against her face. Eve asks Adam, "What are those little spots of light way up high?" "They are called stars, I do not know what they are, but they are called stars. We will have to ask Michael." Eye lids become heavy, and both drift off into pleasant dreamy sleep.

CHAPTER 8
Sweet Fruit Turns Sour

As the first sliver of the Sun peaks over the horizon eye lids on Adam and Eve begin to halve. As to Sun grows brighter, the eyes grow wider. With a stretch, Adam sits up, and looks at Eve, her head still on her pillow. "Good morning beautiful Eve, do you remember me?" "Of course I do, silly. Adam, we were made for each other."

Adam walks a ways into the thicket. He shakes a few branches and returns with an armload of fruit and nuts. The bigger fruits he breaks in half, and he shells the very easy to shell nuts, and serves Eve breakfast. A large leaf from an Elephant plant serves as a tray;

the lovely couple enjoys their very first breakfast on the newly created planet.

Shortly after breakfast Michael arrives with a number of angels. Eve sees them and thinks, "I never imagined there could be so many just like us. Look Adam," Eve holds up eight fingers. "There are this many people beside Michael and you and I." Adam pointing, and touching each finger counts, "One, Two, three, four, five, six, seven, and eight, that is how many others have come. I think they are called angels."

Michael introduces Adam and Eve to the eight angels that have come with Him. Then He leads the group to a place where the ground forms some nice seats in a half circle shape. Michael calls on one of the angles to lead in singing. The angels know all the songs, but singing is new to Adam and Eve. First the angels sing while Adam and Eve listen. Then the angel suggests they sing the same song again and Adam and Eve can join them in singing. Adam and Eve don't sing as well as the angels, but it makes them happy, Eve even more so, "I like to sing."

After singing a while, one of the angels stands before the seated group. The angel tells of his personal experience. "God, that is the Father, the Son and The Holy Spirit make up the sovereign God. Eve, you were surprised to learn that there were eight others just like you. Well, Eve there are billions and billions of angles plus billions of beings like you that are not angels. God has created the most beautiful places for us to live. There is much that I can tell you about God, but this one thing I like best."

"God could have made us to just follow His orders and we not know that any other alternative exists, but He did not do that. God gave us freedom. We all have independent free thinking brains. We can do as we like. One might think, What is the difference? We do everything according to God's will anyway. Well, we learn that the character of God is love, compassion, respect and concern for others. His way is accurate, proper and it works. He does not order us to do right, He teaches us. If Michael tells you something, believe me it is the right thing. You will want to know why. That is fine. Michael will teach you all the reasons why, but be patient, you cannot learn everything in one day, in fact learning will continue forever."

"You will need to know that there is one trouble in the cosmos. There is an angel that promotes his own way. When I was dealing with Lucifer's accusations against God, I thought all Lucifer says may be so, but God and Michael have been so wonderful to me, I have never experienced anything unpleasant from them. I have decided to remain loyal to the Father, Michael the Son and the Holy Spirit. There has been rebellion in heaven and Lucifer and those that have joined him, of which there are billions, have aims on destroying all that God has. To insure our freedom Michael has trees of The Knowledge of Good and Evil in many various places for Lucifer to be able to communicate his opinion.

"Eve excitedly asks, "You mean someone wants to destroy the beautiful garden? Adam, what is this tree of knowledge of good and evil? Did you know about this? You did not tell me." "Eve, I knew about the tree, but the Father, Holy Spirit, Lucifer and a rebellion I know nothing. Jesus what does all this mean?"

Michael explains, "the Father, and Holy Spirit, creation, heaven, Lucifer, all that has happened and the creation of this Earth." Adam and Eve do not learn everything at one time but they understand more. Eve says, "All this makes me uncomfortable, can we sing some more, singing makes me happy." "In deed," the angles teach Adam and Eve to sing more songs.

Angels go off into the garden, and gather fruit that even Adam has not yet tasted. Adam named all the plants, but he had not yet had opportunity to taste all of them. The group has a very nice lunch together. Then they take a walk about the garden. They come to the meadow where the two trees stand. Walking out into the meadow Michael explains the need for Adam and Eve to eat of the fruit from the Tree of Life. Michael reaches up plucking two fruit from the branches and hands them to Adam and Eve. All the angels take and eat, even Michael eats a fruit, not that He needs one for it is He that put life into the fruit, and He along with the Father and the Holy Spirit only have life in themselves. Even though Adam and Eve learn some disheartening things the day is wonderful with Michael and the angels. The angels promise to return often to help and instruct Adam and Eve. Michael of course He comes every day.

Adam and Eve are on their honey-moon in the garden paradise designed by God Himself. How good can it be? Every day Adam and Eve explore a new part of the garden. The Garden of Eden is called a garden, but it is no small plot of ground, more alike the size of a small country. With thousands of different types of fruit they seldom eat the same fruit two days in a row, unless they want to because they like the taste. Some fruit is high up in the branches of the trees. If Eve says she would like to taste that red fruit way up high, it is no problem for Adam. He simply springs up and with feet against the trunk he reaches arm over arm from branch to branch he ascends to the high fruit. Grabs a couple in one hand and descends, climbing down using only one hand.

Adam has gotten over his initial shyness. He now freely caresses Eve and kisses her frequently. They are the happiest couple to ever honey-moon, in the best place to have a honey-moon. They are the first couple to ever honey-moon.

Every day as the Sun is approaching sun set, Michael joins them for a little walk amongst the trees, or just sit by a river. Michael tells them about the history of eternity. How He, The Father and The Holy Spirit cooperated in creating the stars, planets and the Sun. That in heaven, His primary home there are billions of angels. Some of those angels from time to time come and visit with Adam and Eve as well.

Michael tells them all about the problem in heaven. That heaven is now divided into two separate cities on different planets. There is the loyal city, which is twice as large as the rebel city. Lucifer, the leader of the rebellion was the highest ranking angel, being free, as all the angels are, and intelligent, he chose a way outside of love. God sent Lucifer and his followers from heaven, but God made a way for him to communicate with all the loyal angels and beings of other planets. God could not just deny Lucifer's accusations, but has to let them ripen so everyone can see Lucifer claims and what God really is and what He teachers is the only happy way of life.

"This is why there is a Tree of The Knowledge of Good and Evil. Lucifer can come to you and tell you of his claims only at this tree. He will try to get you to eat fruit from that tree, but do not do so. Eating that fruit will only bring unhappiness."

At the same time, on the planet Bottomless Pit. Lucifer and the rebel angels are discussing their next step. Lucifer says, "The Creator God is forgiving by nature. He will not let Adam and Eve suffer the consequences of a rebellious act, He will forgive them. My plan is to trick Adam and Eve into disobeying God's instructions. Once they listen to me, I will cause them to mistrust God. When they mistrust God they will be in a weakened state, and I will convince them that God is holding out on them. They will think to gain that which they are missing, causing them to disobey. God, as his character is, will exude loving forgiveness, and we will present ourselves with Adam and Eve and be forgiven along with them."

All the other rebel angels agree with Lucifer that God is gracious, loving and full of forgiveness, so the plan sounds like their best option. Legion speaks up, "We are all in agreement with you on your plan, but how are you going to do this?"

"I will morph myself into a Seraph. They will recognize me as a serpent. Adam already named such animal as a serpent. I can only communicate with them at the Tree of The Knowledge of Good and Evil, so I will go to the tree and wait for one to come near. Eve, has learned to lean on Adam, and trusts him, maybe I can, more easily, get her to trust me."

Lucifer morphs himself into a Seraph, and descends to Earth, landing in The Tree of The Knowledge of Good and Evil. He cannot see Adam and Eve all the time, for they are off in various parts of the garden. Sometimes while Adam is up in the tops of the trees, Eve is seen in the meadow. "Oh, Yes," Lucifer thinks to himself, "Yes, Darling Eve, venture a little closer, and I will have you in my clutches." But Eve is intent on Adam, and is oblivious to the danger lurking in the forbidden tree. Lucifer is marooned in The Tree of The Knowledge of Good and Evil for days and weeks and months with nothing, but forbidden fruit to eat. He is getting tired of the same food day after day. Besides even in his serpent being form, lying on these branches is not the most comfortable.

Over the months Adam and Eve come into the meadow. They come to eat a little fruit from the Tree of Life. They come together, arm in arm, sometimes singing, sometimes dancing, but always skirting The Tree of The Knowledge of Good and Evil at the greatest distance possible.

One day, as fate would have it, Adam is up a humongous tree, even out of the sight of Eve. A very large beautiful butterfly comes fluttering along. Eve is enthralled by the butterfly, and follows it in flight. The butterfly is ignorant of danger, and flies innocently into the branches of the forbidden tree. Eve's captivating attention on the butterfly makes her oblivious as to her wonderings. She is now in the shadow of the tree she was told to avoid. "Eve, my darling daughter," she hears, turning to see, sees nothing, and having only heard the voice of Adam, Michael and some angels, she brushes it off as maybe just the sound of the wind. Before she can make a correction on her course, the voice speaks again. "Eve, my darling daughter, how beautiful you are today." "My, whoever it is, they call me daughter, they must be from heaven for Michael calls me, 'my daughter, Eve.'" "Eve, I am up here." Eve looks up into the boughs of the tree. There he is, a serpent. "How is it possible," she speaks out loud, "the other serpents cannot speak, in fact no animal can speak?" "I could not speak either, but I was fortunate to stumble serendipitously onto this wonderful tree and its magical fruit for as soon as I ate the very first one I was able to speak." "I am amazed that you can speak and that you are still alive, God said that if Adam and I eat of this tree's fruit we will die. We are not to eat it or touch it" "Yes, but God knows that you will not really die, but he is keeping some marvelous aspects of life from you for when you eat this fruit your eyes will be opened and you will be like God, knowing good and evil." The serpent then picks a fruit and drops it down to Eve. Her reactions are very quick, and she easily catches it. "You see, touching the fruit has caused you no harm, but just touching the fruit, you do not get the marvelous blessings. To receive the complete blessing you must, as I did, you must eat the fruit. Go ahead; a little fruit never hurt anyone." Eve looks at the fruit in her hand. "The fruit is in my hand, but I will not eat any, I will just smell it." She raises the fruit to her nose and takes a sniff. "The serpent picked a ripe one, this does smell very delightful." "The taste is even better than the smell, you will never know until you try." "Oh, perhaps you need Adam to assist you to make a decision; I can understand that you need Adam to do your thinking for you." "He is only a few hours older than I am. I am quite capable." "Then what is the cause of your indecision?" With that Eve defiantly takes a bite. "Do not stop there, here is one from the top on the tree, it is sun ripened, you will love it." Eve takes and eats the second fruit. Eve feels a sensation go through her body like she has never felt before. She believes it to be the effects of the fruit, but it is probably a hypnotic trick of Lucifer.

"I am sure you will want to share this wonderful blessing with your loving husband, Adam. Here let me help you, I will pick some the best fruit for you to take to him." The serpent loads Eve up with an arm load of the fruit. Eve leaves, retracing her steps back to where she left Adam. Adam drops out of the tree with an arm load of his own fruit.

"Here, Eve, you will enjoy these, a fruit we have never tried." Adam then notices Eve with her arms full of another fruit that he has not seen before. "What do you have Eve, and where did you get them?" "I got them from the tree in the meadow. Would you believe, a talking serpent gave them to me. He said that eating them would make me wise, and he was right. I want you to eat some too, here have one." She holds a hand out with the fruit. "Eve, this fruit is from the tree that God told us not to eat." "Adam, honey, nothing bad has happened to me, in fact a zealous elevating feeling has come over me, I loved you before, but after eating this fruit I love you even more. Your wisdom and love for me will be elevated when you eat this fruit."

There is a power that a woman has over a man, a power that does not come from strength, but actually from weakness. The touch of a woman is soft, to look upon her is captivating, and her voice is mesmerizing chimes in the ear. Adam is not fooled by claims that the fruit brings exaltation, he remembers God's words to not eat of this tree, but these words are eclipsed by Eve's feminine charm, and his want to be charmed. He takes the fruit, in full knowledge that eating is an act of rebellion, and eats it.

There is more to eating this fruit than either of them imagine. Adam looks at Eve. "Eve, perhaps it would be better if you did not expose yourself so. You should cover yourself, especially around, well you know what I mean." Adam looks down at himself. "Ah." "That's right Adam, you are naked just like me." The leaves of this tree, what do you call it? Oh, Yes, fig tree. The leaves are soft and we can string them together using grass. I learned this fixing my hair, I call it braiding. We can braid grass and make a belt to go around our waist to hold the leaves. They sit down and work together to make the aprons. Eve ties one on Adam, and asks him to tie hers in the back. "Now isn't that better?" "Yes, but I think you need even more than I." Adam sits down and make Eve a necklace with leaves in the front. "Here, try this on." Eve puts on the necklace and now her upper torso is clothed as well.

"I do not know if I love you more because of apple eating for I loved you more than life itself all along. Everything seems to be the same, you are lovely as ever, the birds are singing, the garden is still a wonderful place. Only that we need clothes is different, and... also, what will happen when Michael comes, will he be angry with us?" "The serpent said that Michael is keeping the full virtues of life from us. I still do not understand just what we were missing." "We will not have long to wait to find out how Michael feels about our disobeying him for He will be here shortly."

Sure enough the usual evening time of the day, Michael begins walking in the garden but Adam and Eve do not greet Him as usual. Adam daily enthusiastically greeted Michael as this time with Michael was the highlight of his and Eve's day. The sound of Michael's voice breaks the uncomfortable silence as Adam and Eve crouch behind an elephant leaf plant.

"Adam where are you." Adam thinks, "How can a voice be so melodic, tender, loving and still be so powerful as to shake the very tree I am hiding behind?" "I am sorry, Michael, my God and maker. I am hiding because I am afraid. I am naked." "Adam, who told you, you are naked? Did you eat of the tree that I told you not to eat?" "Dear Michael, a strange thing happened to me. The woman that you gave to be my companion, she gave me some of the fruit. She was so compelling, that I could not bring myself to say no to her, so I ate some of the fruit." "Eve, did you do this?" "The serpent that I met in the tree used very tricky words, and hypnotic powers to dupe me into believing him. I ate and I gave some to my husband."

Lucifer in the form of the serpent is still in the tree. Michael calls to the serpent to come down from the tree. The serpent refuses. "I cannot for you have limited my access to the forbidden tree." "You and I both know that those conditions no longer apply on Earth, come down." Lucifer still in the form of a serpent comes down. Michael first addresses the secondary character in this plot, the serpent. "Serpent, you are the most gifted of all the animals, but I will make you the least, for a curse will be upon you. You will no longer fly, but will crawl on your belly. You will eat the dust of the cattle's hoof, and all animals will loath you."

God had power to restrain Adam from going near the forbidden fruit; but this action on God's part would give Satan cause to sustain his accusations, that God is arbitrary in His rule. Man would not have been a free moral agent, but a mere robot.

Michael now turns His attention to the primary character, Lucifer. "I will put antagonism between you and the woman." This on the surface sounds bad, but when Adam and Eve complied with the words of Lucifer they turned over their jurisdictional powers to Lucifer. This antagonism that exists shows that Lucifer does not have complete mindless control over mankind.

Through man's act of distrust in God by trusting in some other alternate intelligence, mankind lost their freedom. Adam and Eve and all their children became slaves, and children of God are not slaves. All that follow Lucifer (Satan) are slaves. Lucifer gained control over the human race and ruler ship of the Earth. But, Michael makes a way for humanity to cast off Lucifer's yoke of bondage, but the shackles of slavery do not vanish overnight. The lack of trust in God got mankind in trouble, so mire trust in God's salvation to redeem lost children is all that is required, breaking mankind loose of Lucifer's curse of death, and begin the children regaining the attributes of love, the love that is the foundation of God's government. Through the sacrificial Son, that would come, Adam and Eve and all their children regain the power to again become the children of God.

This antagonism and promise of empowerment did not stop with Adam and Eve, but is hereditarily past to their posterity.

Michael goes on to say that the two in this struggle will be wounded. One will be seriously wounded and the other fatally so. "In this conflict, you, Lucifer will have your head crushed, but in the process you will inflict a serious wound to the promised seed of the woman, you will bruise his heel."

Every one present is personally involved in this conflict, so no one will escape suffering, and savage abuse.

Adam and Eve understand that one of their children will come and overcome Lucifer, and deliver them back to their former relationship with Michael and the God Head. This is a most inspiring reassurance of restitution by which Adam and Eve maintain their hope and courage for the future. As children are born to them, they share all their experiences in the garden, with Michael and how they foolishly lost all, but how through the promised one all will one day be regained.

Adam and Eve, are still clad only in a few flimsy leaves. By their distrust, they lost their robes of Michael's righteous character. Being thusly clothed is a symbol of having a righteous relationship with God. God thusly makes for them alternate clothing from a source symbolic of how their original heavenly ward robe can be regained. Michael makes clothes for them out of lamb skin. The killing an innocent lamb, is symbolic of the Lamb of God, that will take away the sins of the world.

Adam and Eve are evicted from their garden home. The Garden of Eden is a superb place unequalled by any place on Earth. Outside the garden the ground is of diminished fertility and thorns are enabled to grow on some plants. Adam and Eve do not move off to a barren desert. The land is still lush with vegetation and the plants that Adam cultivates grow quite well, though he now must work much harder, and God adds to their diet plant parts like leaves and stems, called vegetables.

The temperature is still quite comfortable, and there are no hurricanes. If there are earthquakes they are rarely of any consequence as there are no buildings to fall on them. They do need clothing for warmth, but for modesty. Eve is already good at braiding, so she soon learns to weave plant fibers like flax and cotton, and the fleece from sheep. Her techniques improve over time and soon she is making cloth to make clothes.

Adam and Eve believe that one of their children will someday solve their mistrusting problem and restore them to life in Eden. Their first child born is a boy; they name him Cain. Adam and Eve are in hopes that this boy will be the one. The second boy is named Able. Eve gives birth to girls as well.

Michael taught Adam to perform a certain ceremony to teach him and his family about the inevitable results of departing from the instructions of God. God's ways lead to life, happiness and love. Any deviation from God's plan leads to unhappiness, misery and untimely death. To remind the human family of this Michael has Adam take a sharp rock and rub the rock against the neck of a young lamb. What a shock to Adam the first time. Blood starts to run out from the cut on the lamb's neck. Then the lamb becomes weak and falls to the ground, then stops breathing. Adam tries to help the lamb back to its feet, but unbeknown to Adam the animal is dead, no longer living, it just limply falls again to the ground. There are ways of living that come into the minds of men, but all of them end in disappointment, misery and death. Life outside of God is only death in disguise. Only the way of God is life, not because God is a dictator, but because only a life based on love will insure the wellbeing happiness and life of the family of living creatures. The dead lamb is laid on a stack of rocks, Adam prays and fire descends and consumes the lamb.

Adam performs this ceremony routinely, and tells his children all the history and the meaning of the ceremony.

Adam's two sons continue to do the same when they became of age. Cane, the elder son is a farmer, and Able tends sheep. The requirements are to kill a lamb and burn the body on a rock table or alter. Cane gets it in his mind to do things his way. Always when a person determines to conduct their life in a way other than the way God directs the results are devastating.

Both sons build alters according to the instructions, but Cane presents to God fruits and vegetables from his labors. Able on the other hand brings some fruit, vegetables, grain and he also brings a lamb. On previous occasions when Adam conducted the offering, he laid the lamb on the alter. Adam would step back and God would send down a bolt of fire and burn up the lamb, fruit and grain. This time fire comes down and burns up Able's offering, but nothing happens to Cane's. This makes Cane very angry.

God, that is Michael, even comes especially to talk to Cane to try to get him to understand. "If you do the right thing all will be well with you. I care for you as much as I care for anyone else. I am only asking you to do a small thing, do it and you will be accepted and you will have no reason to be angry."

Cane listens to God, but argues in his mind. He would think about God's advice, and then pride would fill his mind and he would think I want to do it my way. With no plan, plot or even an idea of harming his brother, Cain sees Able in the field, and the sight of his brother, Able, makes him so angry that he runs over to Able grabs Able's Shepard's cane from him and strikes him. Able moves back raising his arms to protect himself, but Cain strikes again and again until Able falls to the ground. Cain strikes Able even more until he is as limp as a lamb in the sacrifice offering, he is dead.

Something happened to mankind when Adam and Eve distrusted God, who they had known all their lives, but trusted Lucifer (Satan) whom they had only known for a few minutes. Satan became the emperor of this planet. Satan acquired great power over humans, however, they retain, though greatly diminished, their individuality, and freedom, that is power to think and do. God makes available the Holy Spirit and Angels to all mankind, and to those who request help, God doubles up on this protection. Michael gives to man the power to cast off Satan's hand cuffs, but the anger of Satan continually tries to put them on again and again.

CHAPTER 9
The Second Adam

Though there has been perhaps twenty to twenty-five billion human beings to have lived or now living, the Earth has only had two men to ever live on it, Adam, the first man, and Jesus Christ, the second man. Adam was subject to temptation, but he had such a close personal relationship with God that his desire was only to trust and follow God. That was until his love for Eve superseded his love for God, and Adam departed from trusting in God.

All other men subsequent to Adam still have an innate desire to know and follow God, but they also have some what the nature of Satan. Such characteristics as; self-centeredness, greed, and over whelming desires have plagued man throughout Earth's history. Adam's first son, because he could not have his way, killed Adam's second son. Since then, billions have been killed at the hand of fellow family members.

The promised seed, or child, is the second man. The second Adam or man was subject to much more temptation than was the first Adam. Contrary to evolutionary theory man has not been evolving to greater body strength and mental superiority, but in fact has declined. Man's life is shortened, his physical strength lessened, he is subject to a myriad of ailments, and his IQ is diminished. To this situation comes the second Adam, the second man, the promised seed, Jesus Christ the son of God.

The Bible says, "A body you have prepared for me." Michael is the one that said that. The body was prepared for Him. He put down His Godly body, His sovereign position, and palace environment to become a subservient child in the ghetto. Jesus is Michael in human form.

The little planet, Earth is the lesson book for all of God's creatures, both Earthly and Celestial. Angels and the beings of other planets have been watching as Earth's history has been developing, and with keen interest did they follow every event in the life of Jesus Christ.

The book of Daniel told the time of arrival of the Messiah, that is Jesus. When questioned about such a time, the temple priests knew that the time for the messiah was at hand.

Jesus was born into a pour family. He led a quiet life, and brought no attention to himself. The only attraction Jesus offered was truth, the word of God.

The word, that is, the thoughts of God were action implemented by the life of Christ. He came to this Earth where God's government has suffered a coup. The life of Christ reveals the nature of God, not just to Earth bound humans, but to angles and beings of loyal planets.

Jesus Christ, formerly Michael in heaven, comes to demonstrate God's law of self-renouncing love. This is the love that is necessary for peace and happiness to reign throughout all creation.

Lucifer accuses God of being severe and unforgiving. One third of the angels and mankind fall for this line. This alone is the cause of poverty, misery, suffering and death. A divine claim would not justify God; there needs to be a demonstration to prove God's character.

God designs all life to be a benefactor as well as being a servant to all other life. All life is designed to bring life sustaining necessities to fellow creatures. Only the selfish heart of man is plagued with covetousness.

Michael, the Son of God took upon Himself the life of a servant. He is the one and only example of the character of the God Head. He lived as a man to show us how to live. That life serves also as replacement life for all humanity when embraced by faith, for when He lived we lived, when He died we died, when He resurrected from the dead, we did likewise. His sacrificial execution serves as total exoneration of humanity. He endured the consequences of deviating from God's plan of living that constitutes sin. He took our sins and gave us His righteousness which includes His eternal life. God the Father initiated a complete reconciliation with man in what His Son did on the cross.

Satan desires to separate man from God, but God's plan, is not just to restore man, but to elevate him above angels and all other celestial beings.

CHAPTER 10
The Childhood of Jesus

Perhaps the year is four or five BC Jesus is born. He with his parents are in Bethlehem for some time, for after 40 days they make a trip to Jerusalem to go to the temple to dedicate Jesus. Shortly after wards Joseph is warned to leave and go to Egypt, which that very night they do. Herod, who was after the new born king to destroy him, dies in the spring of 4 BC. Then Joseph is advised by an angel that it is safe to return to Israel.

On the return Joseph decides that life for him and his family would be better in Nazareth.

The sovereign Creator has an enemy, but that enemy is not humanity. The arrival of His son is proof that God will go to any extent to reach and save his deceived fallen children. The heart of God is plainly displayed in His son. That God's thoughts are only peace, protection, patience and mercy. God makes available all the resources of the universe to reach mankind by showing His love to created beings.

God, the father let Satan have free reigns to show his own character. Satan murders the one truly kind humble man, who is also heaven's representative. Satan reveals that his true purpose is to destroy God and all the creatures that He loves. God is the defender. Satan is the accuser.

Jesus reveals the character of God. He puts all others first, even to the point of His own death. The people that only have self as their admiration are in Satan's camp. When all see the clear results of their life choices, both proud and humble will proclaim, "Just and true are your ways, you, the king of saints."

Jesus is certainly a gifted student. His mother is lovingly dedicated, and attentive to His development. She homeschools Jesus. She teaches Him to read Moses, and all the prophets. He learns the law of

God and the further explanation in the writings of Moses. He learns the history of the Jewish people and prophecies of Isaiah, Jerimiah, Ezekiel, and Daniel, and the writings of David. The activity that brings happiness to Him, and fills Him with joy is living to bless others.

Jesus also receives a vocational education as an apprentice in His father's carpentry shop.

The spirits of human beings are supper charged by coming in contact with divine thought, the Bible, with nature and through prayer. Jesus stays supper charged for these three were His constant focus. He stays energized for service to help others. As an adult he says, I come not to be served, but to serve.

"Satan is unwearied in his efforts to overcome the Child of Nazareth. From His earliest years Jesus is guarded by heavenly angels, yet His life is one long struggle against the powers of darkness. That there should be on the earth one life free from the defilement of evil is an offense and perplexity to the prince of darkness. He leaves no means untried to ensnare Jesus. No child of humanity will ever be called to live a holy life amid so fierce a conflict with temptation as was our Savior.

Jesus grows up in the slums. Slums equal to that of any large city on the earth now. It is not fortune, prosperity and ease of living that produces a blameless character. The truth is, temptation, poverty and adversity in the life educates and refines character. More lives are ruined experiencing success and riches than are ruined by lack, hard times, and even failure.

God appoints work as a blessing, and only the diligent worker finds true glory and joy of life. Throughout His life on earth, Jesus is an earnest and constant worker. We are happiest when we have useful work, society is benefits, and your nation enjoys prosperity.

"Jesus is misunderstood by His brothers because He is not like them. His standard is not their standard. In looking to men, they turned away from God, and they did not have His power in their lives. The forms of religion which they observed could not transform the character. They paid "tithe of mint, and anise and cumin, but omitted the weightier matters of the law, judgment, mercy and faith." Matthew 23:23. The example of Jesus is to them a continual irritation. He hates only one thing in the world, and that is sin. He cannot witness a wrong act without pain which it is impossible to disguise. Between the formalists whose sanctity of appearance conceal their love of sin, and the character of Jesus in which zeal for God's glory is always paramount, the contrast is unmistakable. Because the life of Jesus condemns evil, Jesus is opposed both at home and in the community. His unselfishness and integrity induces sneering remarks. His forbearance and kindness are believed cowardice." (E.G. White, *Desire of Ages p.60*)

Jesus grows into manhood. He lives a quiet life working in His father's wood working shop making various items out of wood. Furniture, cabinets, window and door frames were probably His specialty. His unselfish service to his family and neighbors probably goes unnoticed for He serves others in the most quiet unassuming manner.

Thirty was the Israeli customary age for a young man to take an active part in the ministry. Because of this it is believed that Jesus began His three and one half year ministry at that age. The Bible in Luke 3:1 says, "Now in the fifteenth year of the reign of Tiberius Caesar, that John the Baptist began his work by the Jordan river, preaching and baptizing." Tiberius Caesar began to reign 14 AD. Fifteen years latter would have been 29 AD. Because ways of calculating ages and anniversaries that exact date cannot be nailed down, so approximately 27 to 29 AD John began his ministry.

CHAPTER 11
Jesus, The Healing Preacher

The morning comes when Jesus does not report to work at the family business. He says goodbye to His mother and walks to the Jordan River, only about twenty miles distance. He arrives at the river and sees a fairly large group of people gathered along the shore. Jesus joins the crowd and listens to john's sermon.

He hears John call some of the temple priests, snakes in the grass, and he tells them to start living the righteous life thus represent God in truth. He hears the people ask, "What shall we do?" John tells them, "if you have possessions and someone has none, give part of your possessions to them." To IRS agents

John says, "collect only the legal tax." Roman soldiers were there. John tells them, "carry out your duty honestly, and learn to live on your salary." Many of the people were thinking that John must be the promised Messiah, but John says that he is not. John does implore the people to repent, and submit to the baptism of salvation.

Jesus joins, at the end of the line, as the people form a line to be baptized by John. John busies himself baptizing sinners, but when Jesus stands before him the eyes of a prophet sees that here is a person of a different nature. John shrinks back at the sight, "a sinner cannot baptize the sinless one." But Jesus says, "I am here to fulfill prophecy and so are you, do your duty to God, and baptize me."

When Jesus comes up out of the water, he walks to the shore, kneels, to pray. A few, nearby, people hear His words, but all the angels are intently listing. Jesus prays, That He knows the fallen nature of mankind, that sin has obscured man's mind from understanding heavenly concepts. Thus reaching man with divine wisdom will be very difficult, and getting man to accept the free gift of salvation will be no easy task. He pleads with His Father for power to break the shackles of slavery that Satan has shacked around man's neck.

Angels want to immediately go to Jesus to encourage Him, but the command comes that the Father Himself will respond to Jesus. A beam of light shines down from heaven, described to be in the form of a dove, accompanied by the same voice that had previously spoken, the Ten Commandments, "You are my beloved Son, I am well pleased with you." John along with some of the people hear the voice. All see the beam of light lighting up Jesus. Of Course Jesus hears the encouraging words from His Father. The sins of the world may not have been laid on Jesus yet, but for that very purpose did Jesus come to the earth. That awesome weight brings him to despair. He craves approval of His Father, and His Father fulfills the need.

John is previously informed that this scene would be a sign, and by it he could recognize the Messiah. By inspiration John announces, "Behold the lamb of

God." The people that hear him do not understand the words, even John himself does not fully understand. The Old Testament tells us that God Himself will provide Himself a lamb that would take away the sins of the people of the world. God, the Father sent Jesus to the world to make peace, and adopt all the people of the world as His very own children.

The Holy Spirit of God prompts Jesus to go into the wilderness to commune with the Father. Jesus does not eat during this time. He has a special time with His Father just as Moses had a special time with God, on the mountain for forty days, when God gave him the Ten Commandments. Jesus is under God's protection at this time, but Jesus, must deal with Satan, the rebel, as a man, with only faith in God to sustain Him. God withdraws His protection in the same manner as He did with Job. The hedge of protection around Job was removed so Satan could tempt Job with distrusting God.

Satan comes to Jesus as though he were sent from God to relieve His suffering and to strengthen him, and to let him know that the fast is over, and Jesus can now eat. "The Bible speaks of a high and powerful angel from the very courts of the sovereign God that was banished to the Earth. Perhaps you are this angel, Jesus, or perhaps you are the Son of God. If you are the Son of God, command these rocks, that look very much like loafs of bread, into bread." Satan wants Jesus to give proof that He is indeed the Son of God.

Does Jesus trust God, or must He prove Himself. God, the Father, had just forty days earlier declared, "This is my beloved son in whom I am well pleased."

Jesus, throughout His life never was connected with a miracle that benefited Himself. He only prayed for such power to be applied for the benefit of others. Satan uses the same technique on us, bringing our weakness to our attention, and accusing us of even worse sins than we have really committed. He brings us to the worst depression he can, and then makes his destructive suggestion with either flattery, or vile damnation.

Jesus displays that it is better to endure whatever calamity Satan inflicts on you than to deviate from the protected path of God. Jesus responds, "Man shall not live by bread alone, but by every word of God." Our understanding of the real issues at stake are clouded and obscured by Satan's psychological deception. Sin is reduced to stubbed toe, when the real consequence is mortality. Jesus restrains indulgence, depriving His body of life sustaining nutrition, while we gratify cravings of pleasure and addiction. Jesus' example shows that righteous intellect must rule and not run away appetite and passion. At stake, is our temporary earthly life and health, and much more serious is eternal life, for those who walk on the protected path of God's principles of self-control.

On previous occasions when Jesus and Satan met, Jesus went by Michael and Satan by Lucifer. Jesus was the general of the angels, and Lucifer the captain. Now Satan holds the higher rank. Satan grabs Jesus by the arm and flies Him several miles, from the wilderness to Jerusalem. Satan places Jesus on the very highest point of the roof of the temple. Satan tells Jesus, "I know that you have faith in God, but you know that faith without corresponding action is dead. If you really have faith in God's protection, and you are the Son of God, then put your faith into action. God's own word says, 'He shall give His angels charge concerning you: And in their hands they shall hold you up, and not let you at any time crush your foot against the cement.' So go ahead, jump."

Just as with us, Satan could not compel Jesus, but he does use the most flowery deceitful deception imaginable. He does use habit forming addictions to enslave people that come very close to compulsion, but even then the enslaved can and have escaped from the addiction of slavery.

Satan quotes and misquotes the Bible, understanding and truth is not his desire for us. Satan quotes, "He shall give His angels charge over you," he left out, "to keep you in all your ways." God will protect you in all circumstances that God guides you into; God does not abandon us at any time, but at times we are out smarted into following evil or a lie. Should Jesus comply would not be an act of trust, but of doubt. Jesus responds with unaltered Bible, "You shall not test the Lord your God."

Satan grabs Jesus by the arm, in another attempt to separate Jesus from His God given mission. Satan flies carrying Jesus, perhaps hundreds of miles, to a high mountain. On the mountain Satan shows Jesus a gigantic 360 degree three dimensional DVD. To the north is Russia with its unique architecture, to the east, the Orient and the ornate buildings, to the north west, Europe, from Rome to England, the art and cathedrals, farther west, America. Jesus sees two thousand years of history. He sees cars on through fares and planes in sky ways.

Satan says, All the Earth and its kingdoms are mine, and I give ruler ship to whomever I choose. True Satan has some power on Earth, but the Earth is not his. The book of Daniel says, "The most high God rules in the kingdoms of men." Satan is offering Jesus an easy way out. Instead of a hard life and the cross, here is a supposed way to regain the Earth. Jesus' mission is regain, not the Earth only, but the hearts of mankind, and he must accomplish that only by witnessing to them the love that God has for mankind, and that by sacrificing himself.

Jesus responds, "Remove yourself from me Satan: for it is written, you shall worship the Lord your God, and Him only, shall you serve."

Jesus is immediately dumped back into the desert wilderness. He is exhausted from lack of food and the trying time He just went through with Satan. He lies on the ground nearly unconscious. Angels that watched the whole scene are now at liberty to come to Jesus' aid. They bring Him food, comforting friendship, and a message of encouragement from His Father. They assure Jesus that all God's creation share the benefit in His victory over Satan's temptations.

After some recuperation, having lost considerable weight, Jesus returns to the Jordan River where John is preaching to crowds of people. At first Jesus mingles, unnoticed, with the crowd.

John believes that Jesus may be among the crowd and tells the priests that He is. They, with their preconceived ideas, look through the crowd, but He looks and dresses like the lower middle class. Jesus steps into John's view, who immediately says to all listening, "Look, the Lamb of God." John expects for

Jesus to announce Himself, but Jesus does nothing. Mingling with the crowd, Jesus talks to a few people as the day passes.

The next morning, John sees Jesus coming down to the river. Two of John desciples are standing near him. John again says, "Look, The Lamb of God, that takes away the sin of the world." Andrew and John immediately follow Jesus, and spend some time getting acquainted with Jesus. Andrew is so convinced that he runs to find his brother. "Simon, Simon, we have found the Messiah." Simon runs back with Andrew to Jesus. When Jesus sees Simon, "You are Simon, from now on your name will be Cephas, which translated means Peter. The following day Jesus gets acquainted with Philip, and asks him to be His disciple. Philip jumps at the invitation, and hurries to Nathanael, and invites him to be a disciple. Nethanael is not so convinced. "Nothing good has ever come out of that city, Nazareth where He grew up." Philip just says, "Come and meet Him yourself and then decide."

Philip introduces Nathanael to Jesus. Jesus says something about Nathanael that surprises him. "How do you know anything about me, we have never met." Jesus responds, "I saw you under the fig tree when Philip asked you to come here." "Rabbi," Nathanael answers, "You are the Son of God, the King of Israel." Nathanael like most believed the Messiah would be a deliverer and make Israel a free and independent nation, but Jesus came to save Israelites and Romans alike free from the bondage of sin.

Jesus, with His five disciples, travels to Nazareth where His mother is busy in the kitchen. There is to be a wedding in Cana, a nearby town, and Mary is on the food committee. Jesus and the disciples help Mary load food on her pack animal, probably a descendant of the donkey that took her to Bethlehem. With loads on their own backs they accompany Mary to Cana.

The wedding party is a many days affair. Being on the committee, Mary knows what happens in the kitchen. "The wine has run out. What can we do?" the other ladies discuss. Mary quietly leaves the kitchen, walks over to Jesus and whispers in His ear, "they have no more wine."

Jesus looks at her with dismay, "Why do you bring this problem to me? This is not the proper time for me to make a display."

Mary is motivated by faith, trust, and confidence. Faith based on, yes, evidence. Gabriel had come to her. She gave birth to Jesus without having intercourse. She heard the wise men, experienced the delivery from the slaughter at Herod's hand in Bethlehem, and for thirty years observed His giving nature. She did not understand everything, but she believed Jesus to be the Messiah, the deliverer. She had faith that Jesus would and could do something about the lack of wine.

Even with Jesus' disapproval Mary tells the men servants, "Whatever He tells you to do, do it." She does not tell Jesus what to do, only for the servants, listen to Him.

Jesus, the Son of God, co-creator of the universe complies with her wishes.

The servants are standing looking at Jesus. Jesus slowly looks up at them. "Very well, fill all those water jugs. When you are finished come back to me." They complete the task and return to Jesus. "Now scoop some out, fill a pitcher, go to the Father of the bride, and pour him a cup."

While the servants are doing that, Jesus leaves the court yard and takes a walk.

The very delicious wine causes a stir. Some know that the wine tastes very good. Others know that there was no more wine. Who brought this wine to the party? The servants tell exactly what had just happened. Jesus cannot be found. Mary had told them to do as Jesus instructed, so attention was directed to her. Mary introduces the disciples, and for the rest of the day, Mary and the disciples tell all they know and have experienced with Jesus.

The party ends and the guests all return to their home towns telling everyone along the way about Jesus and the miracle at the wedding. Jesus is the subject of every conversation.

Jesus gathers the balance of His disciples and begins preaching and teaching in the synagogues. The people eagerly listen to him, and His fame grows, that even in Jerusalem everyone is talking about Jesus.

The time had come for the Passover. Thousands of people make the pilgrimage to Jerusalem every year. Most camp, on the way, and during the stay in Jerusalem. Jesus and His disciples travel with the crowds, participate in the conversations about the mission of the Messiah. Most believe that He would deliver Israel from the Romans. Jesus points out in scripture that the Messiah comes to deliver all mankind from bondage, the bondage of sin.

The first day in Jerusalem Jesus enters the temple. He walks into the outer court. The temple that should be a place of worship sounds like a stock exchange, a roar of clatter and commotion.

People are there from many countries. The rulers of temple will not allow heathen symbol laden currency to be utilized in the temple. Money must be exchanged, at a fee, for the temple money. Sacrificial animals had to be approved by the priests, so most people had to buy an approved sacrifice animal at unjustly high prices. The merchants and the money changers make handsome profits, turning a portion over to the priests keeps the business going.

Jesus stands looking at the unruly scene. At first, none of the venders notice Him, but then one perceives His presence. He can see something in this man that is not present in other men. He tells his partner. His partner tells the both next door. From one man to two men to four, eight, sixteen, and so on, soon the whole company of businessmen have ceased business, all is hushed and gazing at Jesus. The outer court, that had been full of hustle and bustle, is now silent.

Jesus walks over to one of the money booths and turns the table over spilling the coins all over. "Take these things out of here, do not make My Father's house a stock market." He opens the corral gate containing cows, sheep and goats, and with a whip of twigs drives all the animals out of the temple grounds.

Panic sets in; merchants, bankers and priests all run for fear. They do not know who this man is, but there is some felt authority that they cannot challenge. While these men are in dread, all the other worshipers, and the children remain in peace, taking in the scene.

Jesus preaches and teaches to them. Many that remain are the poor, ill and lame. Jesus brings comfort to them all and heals the ill, the blind, deaf, and crippled.

In time some in the runaway crowd regain their courage and quietly return. They can see that Jesus is carrying out Messianic prophecies, but pride compels them to reject Him. Finally some get up courage to speak to Jesus. Among other things they ask Him, "Can you show us a sign proving that you have authority to do as you did." What are they, blind, they just had witnessed Jesus clear hundreds of people out of the temple without resistance from any of them, and the temple is now full of healthy people, and they want a sign.

Jesus answers more than there question, He gives the priests and all of humanity an answer to ponder for generations. "Destroy this temple, and in three days I will raise it up." The literal meaning is all that the priest can grasp, the disciples only gain and understanding after the resurrection, for Jesus was referring to Himself.

Jesus was also saying, You, your body, is the temple of the holy spirit. Like Jesus cleaning out the temple in

Jerusalem, He would also like to clean you, the inner most center of your being. A cleaning that none of us can perform. However, Jesus can do this, but only with our permission every step of the way. Our hearts are corrupted and the cleaning process takes some time. Like the temple in Jerusalem was not fulfilling its purpose, we are not fulfilling our full potential. The cleansing only gets rid of garbage you would be happy without.

That night Jesus had an interesting visitor, Nicodemus. Nicodemus was highly educated and held a prestigious position in the temple. He had heard Jesus speak in the temple as did many of his fellow priests, but many of them wanted to shut Jesus up. Nicodemus wanted to hear more. Fear of being called out for fraternizing with a heretic causes Him to clandestinely meet with Jesus at night.

Nicodemus addresses Jesus as Rabbi, and calls Him a teacher from God, but, even though the thought had occurred to him he did not call Jesus Messiah, the Christ of God. Jesus saw through Nicodemus's facade, but because he saw in Nicodemus a keen mind

He posed a spiritual question. "No one will be let into the kingdom of God without being born again." This, "being born again," is not in the realm of human endeavor, but Nicodemus, being earthly, thought only as an earthling. "Can a grown man squeeze back into his mother's womb and come out again?" The lesson continues, "Your mother gave birth to flesh, but the Spirit of God gives birth to the spirit. "The carnal, flesh, or earthly person had declared war with God." There must be a peace treaty. "Come let us sit down and talk about ending this war, even though you have committed horrendous evil deeds, I will wipe your record sparkling white, clean. Leave your selfish, greed and pride and take up the infinite vastness of the creator without horizons, full unmerited favor and truth. This is the spiritual mind. Love, humility, and peace replace anger, envy, and strife. Not dreams, puffs of smoke, or cyber reality, but significance in seven detentions, reality beyond the wildest imagination of earthy man, full of love and happiness. This is not a repair of the sinful you, but a complete recreating. God will give you a magnificent body and mind dwarfing Einstein.

We must realize our humiliating condition, submit to God and trust in Him. Obedience to the Ten Commandments will not save us. Forgiveness and restoration is a gift from God. If we confess our sins, He will forgive us and sanitize us of all unrighteousness. God does not want our robotic obedience, He wants us to learn of Him, and we will see that His way is right. His Ten Commandments are indeed His way of life, that is love for God and love for our fellow human being.

"Our redeemer thirsts for recognition. He hungers for the sympathy and love of those whom He has purchased with His own blood. He longs with inexpressible desire that they should come to Him and have life. As the mother watches for the smile of recognition from her little child which tells of the dawning of intelligence, so does Christ watch for the expression of grateful love, which shows that spiritual life is begun in the soul." (E.G. White, *Desire of Ages*, *p 155)*

"The only condition upon which the freedom of man is possible is that of becoming one with Christ. 'The truth shall make you free;' and Christ is the truth. Sin can triumph only by enfeebling the mind, and destroying the liberty of the soul. Voluntary grasping of God's restoration of ones' self is the only true glory and dignity of mankind. The divine law that we are brought to embrace "is the law of liberty." (E.G. White, *Desire of Ages, p. 420)*

"God had given a lesson designed to show the origin of suffering. The history of Job has shown that suffering is inflicted by Satan, and is overruled by God for the purpose of mercy. But mankind has not understood the lesson. The same error for which God had reproved the friends of Job is repeated by man's misunderstanding." (E.G. White, *Desire of Ages, p. 425)*

A high ranking man from the city of Capernaum, not far from Cana where Jesus was teaching was troubled by his young son about to die. The man decides to ask Jesus to come and heal his son. On the walk to Cana he decides that he will believe that Jesus is the Messiah only if his son is healed. Getting to Jesus, he asks for his son's life. Jesus has the power of a prophet, like so many of the prophets of Israelite history. "Except you see a miracle you will not believe. The people of other cities believed without asking for a sign." Jesus wanted more than to heal the man's son, but to also bring to him God's salvation. If Jesus could reach this man, not with a miracle, but with truth, he, his family and the whole city could be prepared for Jesus to come and teach. The man knows the truth of Jesus' words, his motives are completely selfish. "Please come, or my son will die," he pleads. "Your son lives," Jesus tells him. Now he goes home, but he is in no hurry, for he believes in Jesus and that his son is healed. He, indeed, prepares Capernaum for Jesus to come and minister. When we learn to trust God, He will exceeding abundantly supply us from his abundance.

Jesus heals, and teaches the truth of salvation for three years. He is known and is the talk of the whole country. He is a threat to the supremacy of the temple leaders, and they are planning to kill Him. On many occasions, Nicodemus thwarts their plans by persuading them to be cautious. Jesus' disciples get wind of these plots, so when Jesus says let us go down to Jerusalem, they say among themselves, "We shall go to Jerusalem and die with Him."

Jesus had raised Lazarus from being dead four days, and this just heightens the Sadducees and Pharisees desire to shut Him up for good.

Jesus heads toward Jerusalem; He acquires a donkey to ride on, symbol of the arrival of the king. People are shouting, and carpeting his path with their coats and branches from nearby trees. The possession continues, and arrives at the temple.

The scene is as He saw it three years before, banking marketing and extorting money from the people. The people were taught that God was pleased by the slaughter of many animals. God was not pleased by the senseless cruel slaughter of these animals. The original intent of the sacrificial service was to point to the Son of God, who serves as the Lamb of God. "Look, the lamb of God that takes away the sins of the world." "…by Jesus' death he might break the power of him who holds the power of death-that is the Devil." Hebrews 2:14

As before, Jesus stands watching the scene. Soon His compelling presents causes a hush to blanket the proceedings. "It is written, My house shall be called a house of prayer, you have made it a den of thieves." "Take these things out of here." Jesus does not have to speak twice. Jesus knocks over a nearby table of money, but he needs not clear the entire court for panic sets in and the greedy priests, banksters and mal-merchants scramble for fear, leaving their ill-gotten gains behind.

Now the temple grounds had only the honest worshipers, the poor, the sick, and the children. Jesus prays and with the accompanying angels, the blind see, the deaf hear, the lame walk and the diseased are made well. Jesus preaches to the crowds, and tells stories to the children. The children gather around Him and some sit on His lap. The whole temple was filled with the sounds of the children's singing.

The priests, having quietly returned, are indignant at the sound of the children singing. They believe it desecrates the sanctity of the temple. Here they were, all along, running a racket in the temple, and the sound of children melodiously praising God is repugnant to them. First they appeal to the parents, with no avail. Then they bring their complaint to Jesus. Jesus says, the children are fulfilling prophecy, "Perfect praise will come out of the mouths of children."

In the hearing of a great crowd, and numerous priests, Jesus taught many parables. This is one of those parables.

There was a certain landowner who planted a vineyard. He built a wall around it, chiseled a wine press out of the rock, and built a large tower, so the vineyard could be watched over. Then the landowner rented the vineyard to some farmers and moved to a distant city. When the time arrived for the grapes to be harvested, he sent a servant with a wagon to get some of the grapes as a rent payment. The rent farmers got greedy and refused to pay. They beat the servant around a bit and sent him away without any grapes. The land owner sent several servants the second time with two wagons, this time to collect the rent and a late charge. The farmers were strong men and overpowered the servants, and sent them away empty handed. The land owner thought, Ok, this time I will send my Son, He well know how to handle the situation and the farmers will respect Him. When the Son came, the farmers conspired against the Son. If we kill the Son, the heir, we can keep the vineyard as our own. When the land owner Himself goes to the vineyard, what will He do"

Jesus directs His question to the entire crowd, but the priests speak up quickly. "The land owner will descend with force and destroy the greedy wicked farmers, and then find some honest farmers to rent out the vineyard."

The instant they speak they realize what they had said. They grasped the meaning of the story and understood, they were the greedy renters.

The land owner depicts God, the vineyard the Jewish nation, the wall around the vineyard was for protection as the Ten Commandments served as protection to the Jewish people. The tower was a symbol of the temple to look out for the wellbeing of the nation.

The priests know the history of Israel. Many of God's prophets, sent by God to collect rent of loyalty were imprisoned, beaten and killed. Now here is the Son and they had been planning His murder for a long time.

Then Jesus points out to them, from the Old Testament, what happened during the building of Solomon's temple. All the stones for the temple were chiseled at the quarry miles from the Temple site. They were pre-ordered by the engineers to the size needed for a particular place in the foundation or the walls, each stone had its designated place.

While the workers were laying the stones for the foundation a stone was delivered. The workers tried to place the stone in one place, but it did not fit, so they tried another, that did not work either. Finally they placed the stone aside, but it was continually in their way. It became a nuisance to them.

The time came to begin laying stones for the walls. As the custom was then and still is today a chief corner stone is first laid, then all the subsequent stones are lined up with that corner stone. This stone that had been in the way all the time was now found to be the perfect stone to be used as the corner stone. The rejected stone had been subjected to the elements with no apparent detriment. But could the stone hold up was the question. The stone was put under a load test by Solomon's engineers. Passing the test, the stone now becomes the most important stone in the building.

The Jews know all the Old Testament prophecies concerning the Messiah. The Messiah shall be rejected and acquainted with grief, and ultimately be the King of saints. The priests could see that indeed Jesus was the fulfillment of all the prophecies for they had intently studied. But to them He was a snare, an offense. They would have moved to rid themselves of Him, right then, but the populous was on His side. They will ultimately fulfill their intent, and just as Solomon's stone was put to the test, Jesus was put to the test. He is the corner stone of the Earth and its people; He alone can support all the burdens of the people of the earth. Jesus is either the sure foundation or a stone to stumble over. To them that believe, the firm foundation, to them that reject Him, a stone to be maligned, rejected, made illegal.

"Those that fall on the rock shall be broken, but to those who reject and rebel against the rock, that rock will ultimately fall on them and they will be ground to powder. Falling on the rock is a voluntary act. Doing so places that person under the protection of the rock. The breaking is more like cracking open, so all the undesirable traits can be honed out. Only the unruly attributes human nature are affected, that is selfishness, greed, cravings that lead to theft, harm, disrespect. Dependence on the rock, that is Jesus, rids a person of sin's guilt, credits a record of righteousness, and starts a learning process toward a Christ like character, full of love, and concern for others, where everyone gives all they have to others. Surprising as it may seem, in the society that God designs, full of love, you, and everyone else have everything.

CHAPTER 12

Resolve over blood and sweat

Jesus tells John and Peter, "prepare for the Passover dinner. Tonight we will eat the Passover together." They both think where, but Peter is quick to speak, "Where shall we make the preparations, we have no house. Shall we spread a banquet under a tree in the garden?" "That would be nice, but no. When you go into the city you will see a man carrying a jug of water." Jesus made it easy for them to find the right man, for men do not usually carry water. "When you find him follow him into his house," which was not really going into his house, but into the court yard in front of the house, a proper place to meet a home owner. John and Peter following Jesus' instructions, sure enough they see the man carrying a jug of water, and follow him into the court yard. "Yes, may I help you?" Peter answers, "Our teacher sent us to ask you to show us to your guest room that we may prepare the Passover for our teacher and is twelve disciples." The home owner says, chuckling, "Isn't that interesting." Chuckling more, "I have been building this upper room for some time now, and just the other day a family member gave me a wonderful set of furniture. You will like this room, it has never been used; all is brand new. How many men did you say?" Finally John speaks up first, "There are thirteen in total." "Wonderful, the room will accommodate you just fine."

John and Peter spend the rest of the afternoon getting everything ready. First they work their way through the very crowded market to buy all the necessary food. On the way back to the house John asks Peter. "Do you think the owner will loan us some cups and bowls, or should we buy some?" "There is a shop near his house we can get some there if need be." "Ok, everything is ready. Should we go and get Jesus and the others?" asks Peter. "No need, Jesus already knows where this house is, and He will bring the rest of the disciples"

Toward evening Jesus and the disciples arrive. John and Peter show them to the room prepared for them. As everyone gets comfortable Jesus says, "I am very gratified to be eating this Passover with you. I have been looking forward to it. What is about to happen to me was determined ages before, even before the Earth was created. I tell you, I will not eat a meal like this again until I eat with you in my Father's kingdom. Eat, drink and enjoy." Jesus told them to eat and drink, yet they could tell that He was under a great weight, Jesus was agonizing over something. The Passover meal continued carrying out all the Jewish traditions. The Jesus took some bread raising it up He gave thanks to God, and then broke pieces off and gave to each of the disciples. "Eat this bread for it is a symbol of my body broken for the salvation of the people of the entire Earth." Then He did the same with a large picture of wine, and passed it around.

Drink this wine for it is a symbol of my blood spilled out on the ground for the forgiveness of all sin.

Keeping with Jewish tradition, in the room was a supply of water and a large flat pan used for washing feet. A servant usually did this, but there was no servant and none of the disciples volunteered. Jesus laid aside his coat, filled the pan with water, took a towel and began washing the disciple's feet. Jesus asks the disciples, "Who is greater the one sitting at the table or the one serving? "The one sitting" they chorus, "but I, the one sent from the Father, has served you. Greatness comes to those that put others first and serve their needs. One among you has decided to serve his self-interest, and has betrayed me for a pot of silver. You will all abandon me this night, You, Peter will have an especially difficult time, but I have prayed for you that your trust in me will not fail."

They leave and walk to the Garden of Gethsemane. All the disciples notice that Jesus is walking slowly and His usual cheerful self is lacking. He is grieving over something, but what? As they arrive at their usual place in the garden Jesus says, "I am overwhelmed with heartache, my heart is about to rupture, I stand just this side of death. Stay here." Jesus walks a little farther with Peter James and John, he tells them to remain there and He proceeds a short distance more falling on His face, prays. "Father, that which you have charged me to do is wrenching my inner soul, is there the slightest possibility of an alternate solution. Father, even if not I remain your dutiful Son, and whole mind, body and soul desire your will to be done."

Jesus then pulls Himself up by holding onto an olive branch, and walks in an unsteady manner back to the disciples, where he disappointingly finds the three asleep. The disciples all waken, Peter stands, reaches out to Jesus, and attempts to support Him. "Could you not stay awake one hour with me? Peter, you must pray, so you can withstand the coming temptation." Jesus then returns to the same place to pray. He falls prostrate on the ground. His body shivers, and His clothes become soaked with sweat, even drops of blood ooze form the pours in His skin.

Sweat mingled with blood drip to the ground. He is becoming evil, the darkness and guilt of billions rebellious transgressions are ripping His soul to shreds. Every Sin, every murder, every rape, every theft, every lie is as though Jesus Himself committed it. He is sin through and through even though He has committed no sin. Satan is pressing down on Jesus, that no human really wants Him. The populous will not do anything to help Him, nor are they interested in His pansy feeble life style. The church leadership is out to kill Him. Even among His disciples one is a traitor, and the rest are too lazy, greedy and self-ambitious to adopt self-demeaning love for others as their ideal. For what is He making this sacrifice? Satan drives home, "If you are successful and go through with this plan you will become so repugnant to God your Father and He will confine you to a fate equal with mine, forever band from God's presence. God, your Father has left you to rot. Angels want to come to your rescue, but God, your Father, has ordered them to stand down, and just watch your misery."

Having taken on the guilt of Satan's rebellion Jesus is crushed by the Father's rejection. Satan makes accusations, "The Father's rejection is total and eternal. That all humanity has and will continue to reject you and any offer of salvation. Humanity is too far gone, they have chosen to follow evil and worship me. The best course for you now is to give up on this feeble attempt to reclaim humanity." The Devil, the landlord of hell, now heaps all the corruption of the deepest hell on Jesus attempting to bring Him to despair and defeat.

Jesus, craving companionship with someone, crawls to olive tree, leaning on the tree he manages to his feet, and staggers back to His disciples, who are asleep again. They have not been praying for themselves or him. They offer no sympathy which at this time He craves so intently. Even in this lack, Jesus excuses their weakness, "The spirit is willing, but the flesh is weak."

"Three times Jesus utters His prayer to be relieved of this huge sin burden. Three times His humanity has shrunk from the last, crowning sacrifice. But now the history of the human race comes up before the world's Redeemer. He sees that the transgressors of the law, if left to themselves, must perish. He sees the helplessness of man. He sees the power of sin. The woes and depravity of a doomed world rises before Him. He beholds its impending fate, and His decision is made. He will save man at any cost to Himself. He accepts his baptism of blood, that through Him perishing all of humanity may gain everlasting life. He left the courts of heaven, where all is purity, happiness and glory, to save one lost sheep, the one world that has fallen by transgression. And He will not turn from His mission. He will become the propitiation (conciliation, negotiator of peace) of the race that has willed to sin. His prayer now breaths only submission: "If this cup may not pass away from me, except I drink it (then I will drink every drop) Thy will be done."

The Gethsemane experience of Jesus was as He endured the death of every man, woman, or child to ever live and die on this Earth. Now, though they clamor for battle, angels stand by immobile by order from the Sovereign God. The angel Gabriel is sent to encourage Jesus, and remind Him of the dire need of humanity, lost, unless He continues to endure, also the eternal surety of angels and other planetary beings is at stake. Gabriel tells Jesus, "Angels and beings of the myriads of other planets are seeing more clearly the lying deception of Satan. Your perseverance in this trauma, Jesus, will destroy Satan, establish freedom and loyalty in the society of intelligent beings, and bring in a reign of peace, for God will be vindicated. By persevering you will bring in righteous victory, not only the Earth, but to all of God's creation."

The turmoil was not lessened, the horrendous weight on Jesus' shoulders remained massive, but His resolve is now to endure whatever the price. This trusting attitude brought fortitude and strength to His weakened human body.

The disciples had been awakened by the brightness of the angel. The commotion of a hundred men coming up the hill now draws their attention. Jesus says, "My betrayer is coming to turn me in." As they approach Jesus asks, "Who are you after?" "Jesus of

Nazareth." "I am Jesus." At this time, Gabriel steps between Jesus and the crowd. The presents of an angel is too much for them. Every man retreats and falls to the ground. If Jesus wanted to escape now would have been the time, but Jesus remains. The angel receives word from heaven to withdraw as Jesus must walk the lonesome valley. Gabriel lifts from the scene and the now somewhat apprehensions crowd approaches Jesus.

Jesus asks again, "Who are you after?" "Jesus of Nazareth." "I told you that I am He. You want me, so let these others go without harm." Judas separates himself from the mob as if he were not with them. He takes Jesus by the hand as a friend, and kisses Jesus on the cheek. A kiss is an act of worship, but this worship is fraud. Judas has already told the soldiers, He who he kisses is the one, hold him fast.

Two soldiers grab Jesus by the arms. A temple servant steps forward with a rope. Peter see what is happening and whips out his sword and takes a whack at the servant. His aim is off, so his strike takes off the servant's ear. All the disciples are inspired by Peter and surround Jesus. Jesus releases Himself from the soldiers, picking up the ear from the ground replaces and heals the ear. "Put your sword away Peter, he that utilizes the sword will be overcome by the sword. You must understand that if I command my father would send twelve legions of angels, but what is about to happen is my Father's plan to the benefit of all. " At this, fear grips Peter, "Run for your lives." They all do just that, run off into the night.

The soldiers bind Jesus' hands behind Him and direct Him down the hill. The soldiers and the crowd rush Jesus down the hill, across the valley and through the empty streets to Annas' home as quickly as possible. Jesus is to be tried before the Sanhedrin, but a pretrial before Annas is necessary to establish the charges. Two charges must be brought, a crime against the state, so the Romans will convict Him, and a spiritual offense making Jesus a heretic, justifying the Jew's conviction of Him. The two crimes to be brought against Jesus are sedition and blasphemy.

Annas asks Jesus, "There is evidence and witnesses that you are setting up a new kingdom, and you are forming a secret society to do just that." Jesus replies, "Recently, daily I taught in the temple, before that in the synagogues of many cities. Even when I taught in the country side, the meeting was open to the public. You had your men at every occasion taking notes of my every word. They can testify as to whether my words are of love and peace or insurrection and war. This tribunal is what is in secret, arresting me and commencing a trial in the middle of the night." Annas is confound and speechless. An annoyed attorney of the court, in defense of the high priest rushes at Jesus and strikes Him on the jaw. "How dare you ruddy speak to the High Priest." "My manner of speaking is completely fitting for a court, and the words that I spoke are the truth, yet, you a defender of the law, use violence and hit me." Jesus could have flashed His divinity for an instant and end the trial by proving His identity, but to accomplish His purpose and save the very men that are persecuting Him, He must humbly endure the treatment. Jesus was going to accept the guilty verdict of the court, but Annas establishes no crime, and orders Jesus to be taken to Caiaphas' home.

On the way to Caiaphas' the guards begin to beat Jesus around. They arrive at the home of Caiaphas where there is a judgment hall, the court proceedings are delayed while members of the Sanhedrin are assembled. This gives the soldiers and others more time to beat on Jesus. They put a bag over His head, and take turns slugging Him, and asking, "tell us, you prophet, who hit you, and tell us who will hit you nest." They hit Jesus in the face, in the mid-section and kicked Him on the legs.

In this beat up condition Jesus stands before the Sanhedrin. Like they could not see his condition, they demand of Him, "If you are the Son of God heal this poor beggar." They had brought several Crippled lame blind to the court. Caiaphas, Annas and other members of the Sanhedrin are in a rage yelling at Jesus. While Jesus, all beaten up and bleeding stands quiet and serine. On lookers and Priest a like can see the difference, an indelible image is imprinted on their minds that latter will invoke conviction that Jesus was indeed the messiah.

Lying witnesses present testimony that Jesus incited rebellion and civil war against the Romans, but being lies they contradict each other, and were shown to be a farce. No charges could be established by these fabrications.

After many attempts to establish bona fide charges against Jesus, Caiaphas, in a desperate fit of anger, "Why do you definitely remain silent against these charges?" In fulfillment to Isaiah's prophecy, "He was oppressed, and He was afflicted yet He opened not His mouth: He is brought as a lamb to the slaughter... He opens not His mouth."

Caiaphas wanting an answer, "I implore you by the living God, tell us whether you are the Christ, the Son of God." The hall becomes deathly silent, all attention is intensely focused on Jesus, ears are swollen to catch every word. Jesus could not decline to answer when the appeal is made to His Father. "You have said." The words were slight, but the delivery had a penetrating impact for glimpse of divinity briefly sparkled in the room. Then Jesus added, "Hereafter you shall see the Son of man sitting on the right hand of power, and coming in the clouds of heaven."

The then present situation is, Jesus having been beaten, bedraggled, bloody, bruised and accused opposite His listeners seated at the judgment bar. But Jesus brings to their attention that this will not always prevail. For they will all witness Jesus seated next to His Father, and judging not only His accusers but all humanity for unforgiven sins. At this Caiaphas blurts out in theatrical rage, tearing his clothes, "Did you hear the accused blatantly commit blasphemy?" The panel of judges unanimously concurs, condemning the blasphemous prisoner to execution.

This execution judgment originated at a moon lit illegal court. The entire, yet selective members that is, of the Sanhedrin must be assembled in the light of day for the judgment to be legal. Known priests that are Jesus sympathizers are excluded. The crowd heard the guilty verdict, so to them, Jesus is a condemned criminal. While the additional members of the Sanhedrin are being assembled Jesus is taken across the court yard, passing through the angry jeering mob, to a jail cell. Two Roman guards take Jesus by the arm and start for the jail. While all are yelling one of the mob approaches Jesus from behind kicking Him in the rear, "sit on this, smack!, you, who sit next to God." Another grabs Jesus by the beard pulling His head down so Jesus is looking up and the perpetrator is looking down, "We will see who judges who." The guards manage to get Jesus to the cell, but the mocking continues. The mob's motive is to demoralize Jesus, but His unretaliatory manner drives the mob into insane rage because they are so ineffectual. They continue with their heated yelling all the jeers they know, Satan brings new ones to mind, and they poke at Jesus through the bars.

Jesus remains unaffected by the mob, but one incident does affect Him to His heart fiber, Peter. Peter was not taking part in the rabble, but tried to remain as obscure as possible. Approaching a fire to warm himself, a woman notices him. She had seen Peter come into the court yard with John, a known disciple, and the look on his face was the look of rejection.

She approaches Peter to ask, "Are you also one of this man's disciples?" Peter is unprepared for such a question. Pretending not to understand, "Excuse me, What are you saying?" The young woman gets a little closer and addresses Peter, and the people nearby. "This man was with Jesus, he is one of His disciples." "Woman, you are absolutely mistaken; I do not even know the man, Jesus." Had Jesus ask Peter to rise up fight off the guards and mob, free Jesus, and escape, Peter would have gone into action immediately, with all the courage of David. But faced with ridicule he became a feeble sheep lacking any virtuous character. At first Peter acts nonchalant about the trial, that did not work so now he tries to join in the reticule. His theatrics are unconvincing, for his true self shows through.

He is called into question a second time, "You are one of His disciples, surely you are?" This time Peter blurts out a string of fisherman cuss words. "Get serious; I do not even know the man." An hour passes, and a relative of victim of Peter's sword whirling, ear severing recognizes Peter. "I believe I saw you in the garden when Jesus was arrested. Your accent gives you away as well, you are a Galilean. You are one of the disciples, admit it!" By this direct accusation Peter flies into a fit of profanity. Peter burst into a violent oration comparing his questioner to the effluent of city excrement. As profanity is propelling from his lips a nearby rooster crows, at that instant, for Peter, time is in suspension. Immediately Peter and Jesus' eye establish communicative contact. Peter would have been more comfortable should Jesus' gaze be full of anger and reproof, but no such look was read, for Jesus only looks at Peter with heart breaking pity and sorrow.

While those standing around Peter stand in suspension Peter's mind races through the last three years of being with the Son of God the savior of the world. His teaching, His insight to living a life according to the will of God, and His complete understanding of the inner character of himself, for Jesus had warned him of his present experience with failure. "Jesus knows me better than I know myself." Peter is now grief stricken with his deplorable display of distrust in the Savior, he is horrified with his own ingratitude.

Peter stands up, kicks the fire spreading the fire across the ground. He shoves his way through the crowd, already dodging burning embers. Then he runs to the gate past the yielding guard, flings open the massive door as though it were a screen door, and runs off into the night.

Day light comes quickly, and Jesus is ushered back into the court room. To validate the previous judgment a quorum of Sanhedrin is needs to approve the verdict at a day light session. The council desires to pry the same confession as was heard at the night session. From the claim of being the messiah they could construe the crime of sedition against Rome resulting in revolt. For some length of time the questioning continued, but Jesus remains silent. To the straight forward question, "Are you the Christ? Tell us," comes an agonizing sorrowful reply, each word laboriously trickles from His lips. "If I tell you, you will not believe, should I ask you, you will not answer Me, or let Me go." Then with more resolve and spirit

Jesus added, "Hereafter shall the Son of man sit on the right hand of the power of God." The Sanhedrin Priests understand fully what Jesus had just said for the Old Testament says the Messiah will sit on the right hand of God. The entire Sanhedrin choruses together. "Are you then the Son of God?" "You say that I am," which is to say, "You speak correctly." Again, unanimously and in choirs coming from the Sanhedrin, "Blasphemy, He is guilty of blasphemy, and sentenced to death."

The mob goes into frenzy. "He is guilty, stone Him now!" The jeers and swearing began again, but with greater intensity. "He is a bastard, the worst scum of the earth." They put a bag over Jesus' head, slug Him, and demand, "who hit you mighty prophet?" Angels stand by ready for action, restrained by orders from the sovereign thrown. Heathen Roman soldiers are the only ones moved by compassion to defend and protect Jesus, or He would be killed on the spot.

CHAPTER 13
The Supreme Night Court

The Sanhedrin had authority to judge in religious matters, but had no authority in civil law. They had a bogus charge of rebellion against Rome by which they planned to bring Jesus' execution, but first a trial before the Roman Governor, Pilate.

Perhaps the Jews did not want to be guilty of killing Jesus, so they employ the Romans, for some three years later in a frenzy of anger, those same priests take Stephen, the deacon and stone him to death.

The Sanhedrin along with the crowd take Jesus to the Roman army headquarters, the hour is still early, so Pilate has to be awakened to tend to the mob.

Pilate's mind set is to have a speedy trial, convict the prisoner and relax having a leisurely breakfast.

What a surprise comes over Pilate when he sees Jesus. He is condemned, but there is no fear or hatred showing though. No criminal has every stood before Pilate with such calm. Pilate's expectations was to hear the charge, pronounce sentence, order punishment and return to his leisure, but Jesus' bearing prompts him to more fully investigate, besides he is not totally ignorant of the person Jesus.

Pilate goes to where he can speak to the priests for they would not come in. "What charges to you bring against this man?" The priests are expecting a nonchalant rubber stamp to their unprovable charge of sedition. They are thinking, "no inquiry, just sentence." They answer, "If He were not a rebel rouser we would not have brought him to you. We have tried Him and find Him guilty of death, trust us, give the order."

More comes to Pilate's mind about Jesus. This is the man that raised Lazarus from the dead, and heals the sick. Pilate asks, "If you have judged Him, why bring Him to me?" "We have tried Him and find Him guilty of execution, but we need the civil endorsement. He incites the people, rebels against Roman taxation and makes Himself a King."

Pilate now turns to Jesus, "Are you the King of the Jews?" "You say it," which is the same as to say, "Yes I am." The Priests hear His answer, and shout out, "you see he admits His guilt to all the charges," and they and the crowd continue yelling. Pilate addresses Jesus, "Do you say nothing in your defense." Pilate was between a frenzied insane clamorous mob, and the quiet, calm, serene Jesus, emanating innocence.

Pilate contemplates in his own mind, "Does this man even want to save His life." Irritated at the crowd, Pilate takes Jesus inside. "Tell me, are you the King of the Jews?" Jesus asks Pilate, "Is this question motivated by your own desire to understand heavenly truth?" Pilate understands the question, but pride keeps him from acknowledging, or even suggesting that may be Jesus really is from God, so he says, "Am I a Jew? The leaders of your nation condemn you." "My kingdom is not like any on this planet, nor will it be set up by war like conquest. The foundation of my kingdom is truth." Pilate sincerely wished to know the truth as he asks, "What is truth?" At that very instant the mop burst into an uproar, Pilate is compelled to tend to their clamor.

Arriving before them Pilate announces his judgment, "I find no fault in Him what so ever." Here the object of the priests for years has been this hour, the hour of the condemnation of Jesus, and the civil authority finds no fault at all. "Pilate, Jesus of Nazareth is an enemy of the state, and any one befriending him becomes an enemy of the state as well. Caesar will deal as swiftly with Jesus as with any rebel, and likewise with all who associate with Him." Pilate knew that the Priests would send reports to Rome; true or not he would have to answer to them. This he wants to avoid. The priests unwittingly offered him a way out. "Hmm, Jesus is from Nazareth, He is a Galilean, Galilee is under Herod's jurisdiction." Pilate forms a detail of soldiers giving them orders to take Jesus to Herod. Through the angry chaotic mob the soldiers make their way.

Herod is very happy to meet Jesus. He believes that Jesus could be John, whom he beheaded, come back to life. If he saves Jesus his conscience could be cleared of the death of John, besides he is curious to see a miracle. Jesus arrives with the mob, and immediately the Priests start yelling out their charges against Jesus. Herod orders silence, and the removal of the hand cuffs. "What have you done to this poor man; why is he so bruised and beaten?" "He resisted arrest." "Liars."

Herod orders that some crippled and main people be brought in. "Jesus here is a chance for you to prove yourself. Heal these lame before you, proving your innocence and I will free you. I will assign an armed guard to protect you from these that have beaten you so." Terror struck the Priests, should Jesus heal these, their plans will be completely foiled. Herod continued, "You worked many miracles for the benefit of others, now perform one for your own benefit." This very situation is what kept Jesus silent and inactive for to do so would bring failure to the mission given to Him by His Heavenly Father. While Jesus remains silent, the priests begin to blare. "Jesus is a fraud, He is not from God as He claims, but straight from the Devil, who is the power behind His miracles." Through all this Jesus remains irritatingly indifferently silent. Herod interprets this as callous disregard for His authority. "The priests are right, you are an imposter." At this pronouncement the mob take license to lacerate Jesus, even Herod joins in. Roman guards put a stop to this, so the treatment morphs to ridicule. Jesus is arrayed in a royal robe, and mockingly addressed as a king. To this the Roman soldiers think to be entertaining. The consciences of some are convicted, and turn back from participating in this mockery.

Herod witnesses their restrained attitude, that, combined with Jesus' kingly bearing, he envisions Jesus as unlike any other man. "I will not undertake this extraordinary horrendous responsibility, let Rome. Captain, take the prisoner back from whence you came."

Pilate glumly convenes with the throng reminding them that, "I have already examined the prisoner, no charge is established, and I find Him righteous.

Herod, a man of your own race, is unable to convict Him." Pilate had just pronounced Jesus innocent and righteous, but to appease the mob he proclaims his verdict, "I will punish Jesus and set Him free," an action against his conscience, against justice and against the will of God. Pilate does this, believing that it would satisfy the mob and they will then consent to the release of Jesus. About this time a note is handed to Pilate from his wife. God had sent Pilate's wife a dream, in the dream she saw all the trial proceedings and all that was yet to happen up to the crucifixion. The note in essence said, "have nothing to do with this just man."

From then on all that Pilate tries to do is to save Jesus. Jesus is brought out before the mob again. They immediately begin, "crucify Him, crucify Him" "Shall I crucify your king?" "We have no king, but Caesar." Pilate then, as custom was on this holiday, Passover, offers to release a prisoner. "Who shall I set free, this Barabbas, a murderer, a rebel and, as you say, a blasphemer, or Jesus, who is Christ, that is to say anointed of God?" The mob, under satanic influence, cries out, "release Barabbas, Barabbas, release Barabbas." Pilate, thinking to clarify his question, "Surely your will is that I release the king of the Jews?" "We claim Him not to be our king, release Barabbas." "What shall I do with Jesus, the anointed of God?" Demons mingle with the crowd start a chant, "let him be crucified, let Him be crucified." For some time the uproar continues. When it did subside, Pilate asked, "Why, what evil has He done?" The uproar erupts again, this repeated for several cycles.

The Devil's purpose is not to crucify Jesus, but to get Him to retaliate or in deed to perform a miracle to prove himself. Any of this would have resulted in a failure in His mission to the world, the salvation of man. Jesus' mission is to reveal the character of God in sacrificial love. He could have struck panic fear in army, mob and priests by the show of divine power, but His was not to show God's power, but to show God's love, and thusly save mankind.

Even among this frenzied mob are those moved to sympathy by the strength of character they see in Jesus, many of the priests become convicted that Jesus is all that He claims to be, the Son of God. The very Roman soldiers that had just participated in mockery worship of Jesus were deeply impressed with His kingly bearing in contrast to that of Barabbas. They are convicted with compassion and pity, an experience that they relive again and again throughout their lives.

The uproar continues. In anguish of despair Pilate cries out, "Take Him your selves, and crucify Him, as for Me, I find Him faultless, a righteous example of integrity." "We have a law that He must die, He claims Himself to be the Son of God." Here Pilate already feels himself in the presence of something more than a mire man and the priests say that He talks of being the Son of God, now Pilate is really tormented.

Pilate now goes into the judgment hall to ask Jesus, "Where do you come from?" To this Jesus is silent. "Do you not know that I have the power of life and death over you." "You have only the power that my Father in heaven delegates to you, of those that have sinned here, yours in the lesser." Pilate returns to the mob, "I will let the innocent go free." "If you free this enemy of Caesar you are likewise an enemy of Caesar." At this Pilate washes his hands, symbolic that he had nothing to do with this innocent death. "Mark my words, I find Him innocent. May the one He claims to be His Father judge you in this act?" "May His blood be on us and on our children." Pilate consents to the death of Jesus in order to save his own military career, a mistake he forever regrets.

CHAPTER 14
It Is Finished

Exhausted, deprived of food and drink, beaten and twice whipped, the cross is placed on Jesus's shoulders. He carries the burden for only a short distance when he falls to the ground. The soldiers try to have Jesus carry the cross a second time with the same results. Now what are the soldiers to do?

That morning a foreigner from Cyrene a little town in Libya had just arrived in Jerusalem. While all others would have balked at carrying the cross, this man, Simon did not know what was happening. The soldiers grab him and draft him to carry the cross. Simon picks up the cross, to the sound of jeers and "Make way for the King of the Jews," all in mockery and slander, fills his ears. "This is Jesus, I have heard of Him." Latter Simon learns about Jesus and His mission, this becomes a blessing that lasts all his life, that he had had the honor of carrying the cross for the savior of the world.

The followers of Jesus are in the crowd in equal or greater numbers as the rabbel-rousers, but they perceive that the rabbel-rousers outnumber them because of their continual racket, in fear, they remain silent. In contrast to the majority, some women, may be benefactors of a miracle healing themselves or family or friends of those that were, publicly display their sympathy for Jesus. While priest and mob are blaring angry words, these women are sobbing genuine tears. Jesus has no words of defense to the angry mob, but He stops to talk to the women. "Daughters of Jerusalem best not to weep for me, but for your selves and your children, for worse than this is coming to this city. At the end of this rebellious age men will cry out to the rocks and mountains, 'fall on us and hide of from the one coming to judge us.' If this is what they will do to the Son of God, what will they do to mere man that continues in sin?"

Jesus had told His disciples, "All of you will be scandalized because of me, the shepherd will be struck and the sheep will scatter." The disciples, those that a few days earlier had jubilantly saluted Jesus with, "Hosanna" were now either standing afar off, or joining the mocking mob. The disciples, and Mary, mother of Jesus were expecting that at any time Jesus would display His power, overcome His oppressors, and take His rightful role as ruler of Israel.

Jesus could have His blood melt the steel spikes that were driven into His flesh. He could have transformed the crown of thorns into wreath of olive branches. He could have activated a whole army of angels to come to his rescue, but He did none of these things. Instead He, fore mostly, endured the rejection of His heavenly Father, He endured the unjust trial and execution inflicted by man, and the cowardly abandonment of His closest followers, the disciples.

The prisoners are stripped of all clothing, and secured to a cross. One soldier with iron mallet and an iron stake places the tip of the stake on the flesh of the prisoner and drives it in with a swift blow the stake is through the flesh and into the wood, perhaps one or two more blows are necessary to secure the stake to the wood. The Roman soldiers wrestle the two thieves, binding them to their crosses while the thieves condemn them and their mothers with the most vulgar oaths. In contrast, Jesus gives no such resistance, nor do any unkind words originate from His mouth, on the contrary, as His cross is being stood up Jesus speaks, to the clear hearing of soldiers, thieves, priests, and mob, "Father forgive them, for they really do not know what they are doing." Jesus was earning the right to represent humanity at their trial before the Sovereign Monarch of the universe. This right is recognized by every intelligent created being in the cosmos, even Lucifer, Satan, has no grounds upon which to contest this earned right. The pronoun, "Them," in Jesus' prayer represents all that ever lived on Earth, from Adam to the last baby born as Earth's history ends.

The frenzied mob continues as they had, "If He is the Son of God let Him free Himself from the cross and we will believe Him. You see, He does nothing to our challenge, He is a fraud." To this Satan induced challenge, Pilate orders a sign nailed over Jesus' head, that reads "Jesus of Nazareth, the King of the Jews."

One encouragement comes to Jesus at this time. The one thief that gives Jesus cause to take heart had heard the trial proceedings before Pilate. He knew of Jesus' reputation of doing good. He heard Pilate declare, "I find this man to be faultless, and completely innocent." He is aware of the beatings and mockery endured. The final determining token was Jesus' words, "Forgive them Father for they do not understand what they are doing." He said to the other thief, "We are here because of our guilt, but this man has done nothing unlawful." Then he addresses Jesus, "Lord," (one supreme in authority) "remember me when you establish your kingdom."

All becomes hush at the cross. Within hearing of the cross all ears became cocked to hear the answer to the thief's question. The soldiers throwing dice stop and direct all their attention toward Jesus. No one had ever asked such a question. What would the king of the Jews answer?

Jesus giving the condemned criminal assurance, the same assurance He wants to give everyone says, "Truly, truly, I tell you now you shall enjoy my kingdom with me." Jesus, strapped to a tree, as one cursed of God, is not diminished in divine power, but power to free Himself is not His purpose. To exercise His royal right to forgive sin is His supreme pleasure. His pleasure in forgiving sins has not diminished, all that request, as did the thief, will receive the same answer. "You will be with me in paradise."

Though Jesus is encouraged by the repentant thief He still is in the most agonizing situation that exists in all of creation. Jesus is feeling the anguish that unrepentant humanity will feel when mercy is terminated, when the spirit of God ceases to appeal to mankind to accept the gift of God, and turn from evil. The pain of the beatings and the nails in His flesh are as nothing compared to the torture of being rejected by God, and being infiltrated and enveloped in sin. The face of Jesus was markedly revealed to all. Unlike the unrepentant thief, still angry for the end of his meaningless life, unlike Cain, who in anger killed his brother, and remained angry even after killing him, the face of Jesus defines innocence, serenity, and divine benevolence.

Under blue a sky, a little past noon, without sign of approaching storm, a canopy of clouds, or some light filter forms in an instant. The cross is in total darkness, Jerusalem, and the surrounding area is without the benefit of sun as well. God, concealed in the darkness, comes down to see the suffering of His Son. God extends no help to His Son for the Son alone must endure the consequences of sin. Lucifer is dictator behind Jesus' execution. In being so, Lucifer is revealing his true nature, and God is being exonerated to the entire cosmos. His loving character, and self-sacrificing nature is published and embraced by all intelligent stellar beings, and God is reconciling the world to Himself.

The darkness brings a darkness that shatters the nerves, and hushes every lip, except for the whisper, "now Jesus may come down and take ruler ship." All the people, priest, soldier and child alike clung to the ground in abject fear. The darkness is interrupted occasionally by a bolt of lightning revealing that Jesus remains on the cross. The darkness is lifted after several hours, but the cross remains in a deep shadow.

Bolts of lightning, thunder and earth quakes saturate the scene. The priests claim, "God is displaying His displeasure with this imposter claiming to be the Son of God." Jesus' ardent followers, retreating to concealment, think, "If God has forsaken Jesus, what is left to trust?" Jesus then speaks, "Eloi, Eloi, Lama Sabachthani," which is to say "My God, My God, Why have you left me?"

All of a sudden the dark shadow focused on the cross is lifted, and sunlight shines all around. Clear robust words ring out, heard clear to the city, "It is finished, Father into your hands I command My spirit," followed by a rock splitting earthquake. Jesus' head now lies limp on His chest, He is dead. The Roman officer now speaks the sentiment of a large number standing by, "Surely this was the Son of God."

CHAPTER 15
Truth Published

The truth revealed is the truth about the God Head. Satan claims that God is tyrannical dictator. What is at stake here is; the character of God, His law, the life of all humanity, and the peace and tranquility of angels and all other created life.

God's law is based on love, that is caring respect, looking out for others. The perfection of this virtue was lost to mankind under the influence of Satan. Jesus came to regain all that had been lost. When Jesus stated, "It is finished," The battle had, at that moment, been won. Lucifer had revealed himself as a murderer of innocence, the one who angels and all other loyal beings knew well in heaven as Michael and followed every step of His earthly life. In that life Jesus did nothing that remotely came close to being sin. Jesus' life represents the life of all humanity. When He kept the law, mankind kept the law. When He gave Himself for the benefit for others, all mankind gets credit for doing the same. When Jesus died, mankind died. When Jesus came back to life, all mankind was assured the same resurrection, the restoration of life eternal. Even though Satan's character was revealed, there remains some unanswered questions. These questions must be completely fully answered before God's creation can be secure from rebellion, so the conflict continues on for some two thousand years now, but this conflict will not continue on forever.

Now Satan's new claim is that, mercy, Jesus' death for the benefit of mankind, destroyed justice, and that the law of God is now revoked. This is to claim that God Himself indorses lawlessness and corrupt living. If this were to be true, for what purpose would the death of Jesus serve? If the guiding principles of God's righteous government could just be changed to accommodate Lucifer, Jesus need not have displayed such concern over law breakers as to die for them.

The choice of who we follow is clearly disclosed, each of us makes a choice between these two principles many times every day. Satan promotes; sex as recreation, orgies, one night stands, and the like, worshiping things, people or places as though they were God, making transactions with evil spirits, hatred, lying, discord, jealousy, anger, envious ambitions, violent confrontations (war), envy, and drunkenness. Rejection of some of these, but selective participation in others is still familiarity with Satan.

God promotes; love, (find a definition in I Corinthians 13), joy, peace, patience, kindness, goodness, faithfulness, gentleness, and self-control. Earnestly embracing some of these yet neglecting or rejecting others is still venturing outside God's camp.

In war people die. Satan promotes war even among his followers. When the evil of greed is carried to its fullest, each kills his fellow. God will one day cease holding back the natural consequences of greed and death will reign. God will withdraw His life giving force from Lucifer, and he will parish with his followers.

CHAPTER 16
Your Father Calls You

Two believing priests bury Jesus in a man made cave, with a chiseled rock for a door. The chief priest asks Pilate, suspecting some interference by the followers of Jesus, to have the army guard the grave. Pilate deploys a platoon of Special Forces troops, and places the Roman seal on the rock door to the grave. Had nothing happened that night those troops would still be on guard at the grave, and the seal in place. Satan, as well, wanting to keep Jesus in the grave and dead, ordered his detail of fallen angels to guard the grave.

The night is moonless dark, but the starry night sky is splattered with thousands of bits of starry light.

The guards, may be forty in number, are in place. Two are at attention, spear in hand, at the stone door, several others are standing on the high ground keeping watch, the balance are milling around with about a third asleep.

All of a sudden, the unseen becomes seen. The darkness is vanquished by noon day brightness. The entire platoon takes to the ground as if under attack. The angel that took the vacancy created by Lucifer absence, accompanied by numerous other angels come into view and descend to the earth. The fallen angels assigned to guard duty put up no fight, but flee for fear. The Roman soldiers desire flight, but are frozen in place by equally ominous fear.

All the angels remain hovering while the head angel descends to the ground. He walks over to the two ton rock and moves it as if moving a pebble. Then he wakes Jesus with a message from His Father, "Son of God, come forth, your Father calls you." Jesus has power in himself to take up life again, and prompted by His Father's invitation He does so. Jesus gets up, folds the burial wrappings, dons other clothes provided him and walks out of the cave entrance, all this done, while the earth rattles in a great earthquake.

The same solders that had whipped, beat, mocked and nailed Jesus to the cross are now privileged to witness Him very much alive, and the angels all about. As soon as the angels and Jesus assume on an unseen form, the soldiers, having nothing further to guard run to town stopping only to excitedly tell everyone they meet of their fantastic experience.

Among those that they tell is a servant of the high priest. That servant runs even faster than the soldiers, stopping for no one, arriving at the high priest's door begins pounding on it. Being admitted he rushes to the priest's bedroom, shakes him awake, and tells all that he had just heard from the soldiers.

The high priest, without delay, orders the servant to take all the other servants he can find and go out to the soldiers. Tell the officer to come here to tell me of the news before anyone else can hear of these things. Then he calls for the temple treasurer. "Gather all the coins you have in the treasury. Divide the money into forty-one parcels. We shall offer each man a bribe and the officer a double amount. We must make the amount so enticing that they will agree to take the money and comply with my demands.

The soldiers come to the temple, perhaps thinking that the priests want to know the truth about the Jewish savior, but to their surprise they are confronted with a bribe. To the commanding officer the High Priest entices, "Soldier of Caesar, if you and your men will say nothing further of this hallucination that you experienced, this," handing one of the money bags, "very lucrative reward will be yours. There is a double portion for you and an equal single portion for each of your men. I will guaranty you against all repercussions, if I fail, and your life is in jeopardy, you are free to speak as you will. But for now tell Pilate, and publish widely that as you slept His disciples came and stole the body." The solders enrich themselves agreeing to the terms.

The plan was not very well thought out for how would the soldiers know who had taken the body if they slept through the night?

The high priest meets with Pilate tells his fabricated story and appeals for leniency toward the soldiers. Pilate then privately questions the Special Forces unit. Even though they agreed to the lie and took the money the soldiers are afraid to lie to Pilate, and they tell Pilate the whole truth.

A number of women had previously agreed that on the first day of the week they would return to the grave and prepare the body properly, for the Friday burial was done in hast because of the onset of the Sabbath. They arrive at the grave at different times. Mary Magdalene was first to arrive. Mary sees that the stone is already moved, she looks inside but there is no body. "Someone has taken Jesus, she thinks. She drops her basket and runs to where some of the disciples are staying. She rushes in waking Peter and John. With heaving breathe she stutters out, "Jesus' body has been removed, it is not in the grave."

Back at the grave other ladies arrive. They see the stone rolled back, but a glowing handsome young man is sitting on the stone. In fear they turn to run, but the young man calls out, "Do not run or be afraid.

I know that you seek Jesus, the one crucified, He is no longer here, He alive. Come, see for your selves." They do so, another angel on the inside tells them, "He is alive just as He said He would be on the third day." The first angel peaks in, "Go quickly and tell His disciples all you have seen and heard."

After Mary tells Peter and John they tear out the door and run to the grave. John out runs Peter and gets there first, but halts at the door. Peter, right behind, bolts in without hesitation just to find the rock slab where Jesus was lying to have only the grave linen neatly folded at one end. John then follows, "What do you think has happened?" "I do not know," as Peter turns to leave.

Mary then arrives, now having run the distance twice. Peter and John return home, but Mary lingers. She is teary eyed and not focusing, and her mind is in a daze. She looks in the tomb, two men are there, "What do you seek," they ask. "My Lord, if He cannot be buried here I will find a place for him." And she goes outside. She sees a person coming, perhaps he knows about the body. "Woman, why do you cry? Who do you look for?" Mary starts to answer as she walks closer to the man, "Tell me where you have put Him and I will take Him." "Mary" Now Mary recognizes the voice, "Rabbi," as she lunges toward Him.

"Mary, you cannot detain me now for I must appear before My Father. Go to my disciples and Peter tell them that I am appearing before My Father and your Father." Mary, having caught her breath, and with new excitement, races to the disciples to tell them the wonderful news.

Jesus, as He has just said, flies in a stellar manner to the planet, Heaven. As he lands billions of angels line the road leading to the city. Jesus walks along the road past the cheers and greetings of the angels. He approaches the closed gate to the city where Moses stands waiting. As Jesus nears the gate, Moses opens the gate. This honor is given to a redeemed human. The reception is none abated inside the city. Angels are jubilant for the victory over sin and the salvation of the Earth. Jesus walks up Main Street Heaven, past the city square and on to the thrown of the Sovereign of the universe, Jesus' heavenly Father. "Father did I complete the mission? Is my sacrifice adequate to take away the blight of sin?" "More than adequate, this same jubilant celebration is taking place on all the planets that you created. The exonerated character of the God head is fortified by irrefutable bountiful love. All doubts of my character are vanquished. Unfortunately this rebellion must continue for a time because not all questions are resolved as to the final disposition of Satan."

Jesus enjoys the company of His Father and the whole heavenly population. But He separates Himself from heaven's reprieve to the blight of earthly atmosphere to spend another forty days here.

While heaven was jubilant the believers on Earth are in morning. Two disciples, of obscure involvement, are walking home, a distance of about 8 miles. They are very depressed even though they heard of the ladies experience at the grave, and of Mary actually talking to Jesus, they remained depressed. As they journey a stranger walks near enough to hear their conversation. "What is it that you are discussing that brings you to such despair?" The one named Cleopas answers "We are discussing the events in Jerusalem of the last three days." "What things?" "Where are you from? You must be the only person within a hundred miles to not have heard the news." "We are talking about Jesus of Nazareth, a mighty prophet. We believed that He was the promised Messiah that would redeem Israel, but the Israeli leadership had Him crucified by the authorities." They related all the events of the day especially about the grave being empty and one woman saying that she spoke with Jesus.

"You are not using your minds to understand the prophets for they plainly said that the Lord's Messiah was to suffer many things before fully partaking of His conquering glory." As they walk alone for 8 miles Jesus teaches the prophecies and explains how they relate to the life and death of the Messiah. Clear into dusk they continue the discussion. As they come to their home the two disciples began to slow and stop, but Jesus walks as though continuing on. "No sir," they stop him, "It is late, you surely are hungry and tried. Come have meal with us and stay the night. You can continue on in the morning." Jesus accepts the invitation. The three continue to talk as they fix the meal. As they sit He takes bread in his hand, prays, brakes it and hands it to them. At that instant they see the nail scars in His hands, His gestures are those of Jesus, they look Him in the face, it is He. They immediately descend to their knees to worship Him, but He vanishes from their sight.

"We must hurry back to Jerusalem to tell the others. Grab the bread He gave us, we can eat it on the way." "No, leave it, let us go. I will eat only once I have arrived for I want to run all the way back." "You are right brother, we shall run."

As they made the first trip, so they make the second trip with the accompaniment of Jesus, but he is concealed from them this time. They are running, but this time in the dark. He does not keep them from tripping, but he does keep them from harm. They run, they walk, they stumble, but they arrive safely.

As they arrive, finding the disciples assembled, they convey their experience. "Jesus indeed in risen, we have seen and talked with Him. As they are still reciting all that Jesus taught them, Jesus, coming through the wall, appears to all of them. The disciples are terrified, they retreat in abject fear. "Peace be unto you." Cleopas and his friend are not caught up as much as the others as it is their second time. "Why are you apprehensive and doubtful, see it is me, see my hands and my feet, touch me and be assured that it is really I, myself, in flesh and bones." While they are examining Him, touching Him to see if He really is real, they still remain full of doubts, He asks, "Do you have any food?" Cleopas thinks of the bread that he left on the table, "Oh if I had brought that bread with me, I would have some food to give to the risen savior." One of the disciples fetches a plate with a broiled fish and a honey cone, "Thank you," and Jesus sits down to eat.

"All the words of Moses, the prophets and the Psalms are the words concerning Me. Every description and every event explains My words, My life, My death, and My resurrection." Jesus then takes point by point and explains the scripture.

"Understanding these scriptures will enable you to preach to the world the truth of the Messiah. You will bring mankind to reconsider life's principles, and bring them to a complete reversal of thinking and behavior, thus bring freedom from the addiction of sin, and make righteous living possible. I bring to you the promise of My Father, wait in Jerusalem until you receive that power. This power will bring order, plan and power to the preaching of the gospel. Be filled, surrounded, and inundated with the Holy Spirit of God. Love, bless and pray for those under sin's addiction for in doing so you are helping to rid the universe of rebellion."

The routine of daily life continues while Jesus is on the Earth for forty days. Seven of the disciples go fishing on the Sea of Galilee. They fish all night, but catch nothing. As it is starting to get light a man on the shore yells out to them, "Have you caught any fish?" They sadly reply, "No sir, none." They then hear, "cast the net on the right side of the boat, and you shall catch many fish." They grumble among themselves for a minute, then one says, "What will it hurt? Come on put out the net." So they bring the net to the right side of the boat and, "One two three," the net is flung out across the water, and then the men start drawing in the net. To their pleasing surprise the net is flopping with fish. The more they pull in the more numerous the fish until the last of the net is reached. The net is one solid bundle of fish. All seven men put their backs into the task, and with a heave hoe, but the fish are too many, they are unable to bring the fish aboard.

All are looking at the fish, John then sequences his eyes toward the shore. "It is the Lord." Peter stops what he is doing, "What did you say?" "I said, it is the Lord. The man on the shore is Jesus, our Lord." With that Peter takes a good hard look, "Your are right." Without hesitation, Peter abandons the boat and swims about 200 yard to shore. The others sail the boat to shore dragging the net and fish behind them.

In short order they are all ashore. Once there, they notice that Jesus already has a fire going with fish roasting and bread baking. Jesus tells them to bring some of the fish that they had just caught to add to the meal. Peter, already on shore, walks out into the water, grabbing the net pulls it and the fish to shore.

"Come, sit down, let us eat breakfast together." They have a wonderful time, sitting on the beach eating the bread and fish that Jesus had provided and cooked. All the disciples feel honored and privileged to be eating with God's own Son.

As breakfast is finishing, Peter, being the talkative one, is leading out in asking questions. Jesus has His own questions for Peter. "Peter, do you love me more than these?" "Lord, you know that I love you." "Feed my lambs." All the other disciples hear the question. They think that Peter has forfeited his place as a disciple, because of his deplorable performance, that of denying Jesus. Peter thinks the same. A little time passes and Jesus again asks Peter, "Peter, do you love me?" At this second time the disciples perk up and focus on Peter. "Of course Lord, you know that I love you." "Feed my sheep." "My," the disciples think, "For the second time Jesus commands Peter to feed the sheep. As they are cleaning up from breakfast,

Jesus turns again to Peter, "Peter, do you love me?" At this third time Peter jerks back dropping the plate he is holding for shock of the question and tears swell up in his eyes. The group, now frozen in time stop, breath halted, all eyes on Jesus, then to Peter, all red faced, veins standing out on his forehead. "Lord," all choked up Peter answers, "Lord, you know all things, yes indeed I love you." "Strengthen your fellow believer."

This was done for Peter's sake and for the disciples. Peter thought, he was still a follower of Jesus, but no longer called to be an Apostle for he had failed God miserably. The other disciples had lost trust in Peter, he will let you down in pinch. This was a terrible experience for Peter, but absolutely necessary both for Peter and the disciples. Without this confession Peter could not, would not have been in a position to encourage or up lift anyone. Jesus revealed through this heart wrenching questioning the true confession of Peter and his humility. Jesus, because of Peter's confession, reinstates Peter three times all in the hearing of the disciples. None can deny that Peter has

a commission from heaven itself to preach the gospel
to redeem sinners from destruction.

The former Peter was always ready with a word to
correct others, but now he is called to feed not spank.
Peter, possessing humility, is to reach for deeper
humility, discarding his former impulsiveness, self-
confidence, self-exalting, self, "I will never deny you,"
to a self-distrusting God exalting caretaker of sheep.

"Peter, when you are an old man you will not be
as strong and robust as you are now." Jesus describes
to Peter the end of his life, and how it shall end, how
his very hands will be stretched to be nailed to a
cross. Peter is now willingly submissive, not boastfully
confident. He is mindful of his deplorable treasonous
actions and the savor's gracious forgiveness and
recommission.

Peter then sees John walking along with them,
and asks, "What about him?" Jesus answers him by
saying, "what every happens to him will not be the
commanding influence in your life, "Follow me."

Jesus' last and biggest meeting is a clandestine
meeting on a country hill side with over five hundred

people in attendance. The temple secret police are out in numbers looking for any suspect enemies of the state and established religion. For Christians every communication is on the hush. Word of mouth gets out from person to person that there is to be a meeting on a certain hill probably in Galilee. From all over Israel the message gets out. Many walk up to sixty miles to the meeting place always traveling in twos or small groups. Some people live nearby others must travel a great distance walking.

When coming to the side of the designated mountain people gather in small groups of friends they know. No outsiders are invited, and this is one meeting with Jesus preaching that the Pharisees do not have their spies.

As the crowd is gathering the disciples mingle with the groups telling of their most recent experiences with Jesus.

Thomas relates his unfortunate experience of unbelief, and how he was fortified by seeing and touching. He tells the people of Jesus' comment,

"More blessed are they that believe and yet have not seen as you have."

Cleopas and the other disciple that live in Emmaus relate their story of walking along, unknowingly being taught by Jesus, and how He pointed out all the scriptures in the Old Testament that described all that was to happen in the life of the Messiah. Jesus, the Messiah, the Son of God, is God's way of bringing all humanity back into heavenly society.

Peter admits all his deplorable actions at the trial of Jesus. That after his cowardly denial Jesus looked at Him with such disappointment, but not condemnation that it broke his heart. Running to the place that Jesus prayed in Gethsemane he poured out his heart to God and received forgiveness. How Jesus put him through the humiliating questioning of "Do you love me." That now he understands that Jesus, in the questions, was reinstating him as an apostle, accepted by Jesus and the other apostles.

As the crowd was now fully assembled and the apostles were preaching Jesus appears. He does not appear on the edges of the crowd, but suddenly in the middle.

Jesus announces that the atonement, the reconciliation of mankind to God is fully complete. The way of salvation for all is absolutely assured to all that will accept forgiveness and eternal life as a free gift. That shortly He will ascend to heaven and take the office of the true High Priest of the Universe in the Temple that the God built.

From the universal depository of energy, power and authority Jesus commissions His disciples to take the gospel to the nations of the world. Teach; saved by grace, to love your heavenly Father, love mankind, and obey all that the scriptures teach.

At this very last meeting one of the disciples asks Jesus if now He will restore the kingdom to Israel. The answer comes, "No." "I am not going to take David's throne; a throne that only exists in one dimension. I have come to give you the abundant life, the life that the angels enjoy. You will only understand this abundant life once you are living this abundant life. You will be happy that I withheld from you David's earthly throne when I give to you my Father's heavenly throne.

The Father did not send me to the Earth to save Israel, but to save Israel and the peoples of the entire Earth, and to reveal the truth of His character and the ultimate results of evil. Mankind, angels, and godlike beings on all the planets equally needed this instruction. If people are friendly, witness to them, if people are nasty, witness to them, if they want to kill you, witness to them. Every one, every priest, every politician, every soldier, every renegade yelling in the crowd that tortured me and crucified me is a candidate for citizenship in the eternal kingdom of God."

Whosoever, that includes all, not one human beings is excluded. Whosoever that comes to will be admitted into the family of heavenly beings. Whosoever hears and reacts in trueness of heart to the word of Jesus is the benefactor of mercy and commissioned to tell others. Mankind is weighted down with hardship, weariness, poverty, and sickness, but the source of life's misery is guilt over wrongdoing. The dwellers of Earth believe there are various races of peoples, but this belief only looks on the surface. The heart of mankind is that of a family. There is not a person you meet that does not share a common genetic inheritance with yourself. We are the human family.

Do the right thing, relieve suffering, help where help is seen to be needed, stop harming, stop lying, stop cheating your fellow family member.

Jesus commands his disciples to remain in Jerusalem until they receive the in filling of the power of the Holy Spirit. Then Jesus lifts off from the earth and ascends, only vanishing by being enveloped by the clouds. While the disciples still have crocked necks and angel proclaims that Jesus will again visit the Earth by coming in the same manner that you saw Him leave.

ABOUT THE AUTHOR

Bill Sinock NLA, the Suffix indicates claim to academic excellence, "No Letters of Academia." Standing companion sense high school has been a Thesaurus. His writing goal is to use the least number auxiliary words, utilizing words of precise clarity, emotion and tone, to convey image and thereness. Nothing recommends Bill as an author, but a published author in England, having no arms, must type his manuscripts with his big toe. Nothing in God's universe holds that man back; Bill lives in the same universe, and has arms. As breath continues, so books will emerge.